The Betrayal

A Lifetime of Regrets

BLANCA DE LA ROSA

Contents

CHAPTER 1

ECHOES OF THE PAST—MEMORIES OF A LOST FAMILY

The unsigned divorce papers on the kitchen table were a testament to what she had lost. It wasn't just a marriage; it was the trust and love of her children—a family she had taken for granted. As she stood in the empty living room, the silence was deafening, filled with the ghosts of missed birthdays, forgotten promises, and the bitter taste of regret. Nic had finally reached his breaking point and demanded a divorce. Only now did she realize that she had a once-in-a-lifetime opportunity with her marriage and family, and she didn't recognize it until it was gone, and her life fell apart.

Camila's life after the separation was a shadow of what it once had been. The separation from Nic was finalized, and they agreed to share custody of the children. Adrián, 9, and Celina, 6, too young to fully understand, struggled with the new reality of living in two homes. Camila moved into a small apartment not far from the family home. It was a far cry from the life she had once known, but it was all she could afford.

As the months passed, she slowly began to rebuild her life, but the scars of her affair and the destruction of her marriage remained. She threw herself into work, trying to fill the void left by the loss of her family. Often, she found herself thinking about what could have been, what her life would be like if she had made different choices. She wondered if she and Nic could have saved their marriage if they had been honest from the start. But the past was behind her. All she could do was move forward.

Camila sat alone in her dimly lit apartment, the silence pressing in around her. Photographs of her children adorned the walls; their smiling faces a stark contrast to the emptiness she felt inside. She picked up a framed picture of her and Nic from their college days, their eyes filled with the promise of a bright future. Memories flooded back—late-night study sessions, spontaneous road trips, and the way Nic would look at her with unwavering love. They had been so young, so full of dreams. How had it all gone so wrong?

The weight of her decisions pressed down on her, a constant reminder of the life she had abandoned. Determined to forge ahead, she turned from the window, knowing she must confront her past. Relocating to the suburbs had been a shock to her system. Born and raised amid the pulse of New York City, the hushed streets and predictable rhythms of suburban life imprisoned her spirit. In her desperate search for excitement, she had made choices that now seemed unfathomable. The drinking, the drugs, the endless parties—they had served as temporary escapes, futile attempts to fill her inner void. Each euphoric high gave way to a devastating low, and the excitement she chased only widened the chasm between her and those who mattered most.

Nic had been her foundation, unwavering and devoted, even as she spiraled out of control. He shouldered the responsibilities of both parents, sacrificing his own contentment for their children. Camila's chest constricted as she recalled the countless nights he had waited up, hoping for her return, only to face repeated disappointment. The magnitude of her loss crashed over her like a tidal wave. She had frittered away the love and trust of an honorable man, becoming a stranger to her own children. She existed as an outsider in their world, disconnected from their friendships, interests, and the countless small moments that composed their daily lives.

Camila's vision blurred with tears as she returned the photograph to its place. She had exhausted herself running from her regrets, but now they surrounded her, inescapable. The burden of her mistakes weighed heavily, a perpetual reminder of the life that could have been hers. She made a solemn vow to herself: she would persist in her self-improvement, remain present for her children however possible, and discover new purpose. The path ahead stretched long and arduous, but she was determined to continue forward, one step at a time.

Late at night, in her dimly lit apartment, Camila perched on the edge of her bed, cradling a family photograph. The lamp's gentle radiance cast dancing shadows across the room, reflecting the tumult within her heart. How had she allowed things to deteriorate so completely? How had she sacrificed everything of value? Memories flooded back of family dinners filled with laughter and precious moments shared with Nic, Adrián, and Celina.

A warm summer evening, the backyard alive with laughter and the smell of barbecue. Nic stood by the grill, flipping burgers, while Adrián and Celina chased each other around the yard, their giggles filling the air. Camila watched from the porch, a smile spreading across her face as she sipped her lemonade. "Mom, come play with us!" Celina called, her eyes sparkling with excitement. Camila set her drink down and joined her children on the grass, their laughter infectious. They played tag until they were all breathless, collapsing in a heap on the lawn. Nic joined them, lying down beside Camila and taking her hand. "This is perfect," he said, his voice filled with contentment. "I wouldn't trade this for anything." Camila looked at him, her heart swelling with love. "Me neither," she whispered, squeezing his hand.

The memory faded as she returned to the present. The weight of her decision pressed down on her, a constant reminder of the life she left behind. Suddenly, a painful memory invaded her thoughts: the night Nic asked for a divorce. She could still see the pain in his eyes and hear the finality in his voice. "I've given you ten years, Camila. Ten years of trying to make this work. But I can't do it anymore." He was right. He deserved better. The kids deserved better. And now, they have it. But where does that leave me? she wondered, her voice breaking as she spoke aloud. "I want to make things right. I want to be the mother they deserve. But how do I even begin to fix this? How do I earn their trust again?"

Determined to change, Camila's thoughts turned to her children. The pain of their rejection was sharp, but her resolve to become a better mother was stronger. She knew it wouldn't be easy, but she was ready to try. They deserve a mother who is present, who loves them unconditionally. I need to show them that I've changed, that I'm committed to being better. But it's going to be a long, hard road.

With newfound resolve, Camila made a vow to herself. "I will change. I will earn their trust back. One day at a time, one step at a time. I owe them that much," she said aloud, her voice filled with determination.

Feeling suffocated, Camila called her friend Rose for lunch at the local café, desperate to escape her thoughts. The café, with its checkered tablecloths and the aroma of freshly brewed coffee, was a quaint little place. As she sat there, watching families with strollers, couples holding hands, and children running and laughing, a sharp pang of hurt pierced her heart. The laughter and love around her only deepened her loneliness, making her acutely aware of the empty seat across from her. The café's warm atmosphere seemed to mock her cold emptiness, amplifying her sense of isolation.

Camila saw Rose approaching the café and waved her over. "Hey, Rose. Thank you for being such a good friend and meeting me on such short notice. I just needed some fresh air and someone to talk to," she said, forcing a smile.

Rose hugged her tightly before sitting down. "Of course, Camila. You know I'm always here for you."

As they chatted, the topic of her divorce from Nic surfaced. "I have to admit, I never expected a divorce. I didn't think he'd have the guts to go through with it," Camila said, her voice tinged with bitterness.

Rose reached across the table, taking Camila's hand. "Camila, I know this is hard. But sometimes, we mistake love for weakness. Nic loved you and the kids deeply. He just couldn't keep living in that turmoil."

Camila looked down, unable to meet Rose's eyes. "I thought I had it all under control. The affair, the partying... I thought I could handle it."

Rose squeezed her hand gently. "I know, sweetie. But those things were just temporary highs. They couldn't fill the void you were feeling."

Camila's eyes filled with tears. "I never imagined Nic would do anything but pine for me. I thought he'd always be there, waiting."

Rose's voice softened as she leaned closer. "Nic didn't deserve this, Camila. Yes, he had his struggles, but he's a great dad and husband. He's everything anyone could want in a man."

Since the divorce, her ex-husband had dated several women. Instead of lamenting his past life, he was dating like a single 20-year-old and getting more attention than ever. She had always thought she was the one in control, the one who held all the cards. But now, seeing Nic move on so effortlessly, she realized how much she had underestimated him—and overestimated herself.

"You know, Rose, ever since the separation, I've felt this deep sense of shame. It's like I'm branded with a scarlet letter," Camila began, her voice trembling. "Whenever I see our friends or family, I feel their judgment. The whispers behind my back, the pitying glances... it's like they're all silently condemning me."

"I can't imagine how hard that must be."

"What's worse is that I've lost our mutual friends. They've all flocked to Nic's side, supporting him. It makes me feel so guilty and isolated. They look down on me, and I know they disapprove of my behavior. It's like I'm standing on the outside, looking in at a world I once belonged to, but now seems so far away."

Rose squeezed Camila's hand. "You're not alone in this. I'm here for you, and I know there are others who still care about you deeply. You've made mistakes, but that doesn't define who you are."

"Thank you, Rose. It means a lot to hear that. I just need to find a way to move forward and prove to myself that I can be better."

"Camila, it's okay to feel this way. You've been through a lot. But you're taking steps to change, and that's what matters."

"I've started therapy, joined support groups, and volunteered at the local community center. These small steps are my way of seeking redemption, of trying to make amends for the pain I've caused."

"That's a great start, Camila. It's not going to be easy, but you're on the right path. Just take it one day at a time. The road to redemption can be long and bumpy."

Camila took a deep breath, feeling a flicker of hope. "Thanks, Rose. I know I can't undo the past, but I can choose to live differently from now on."

"And I'll be right here with you, every step of the way."

Camila's eyes softened, a small smile forming. "You have no idea how much that means to me. I've felt so lost and alone. Having you to lean on... it makes all the difference."

Her life, once full of possibilities, had turned into a tragedy. Now, in a tiny apartment, she spent her days reflecting on her mistakes. Camila felt isolated, unable to find comfort in understanding what had happened. She replayed the events leading up to the divorce and the loss of her family, struggling to believe that she had once seen Marcos as her ticket to a better life. That relationship had led to her downfall.

She often imagined how her life might have turned out if she had resisted the temptation of a fast and loose lifestyle, if she had not let Marcos take control. But these thoughts came too late. She realized it didn't matter now, and all she was left with was regret. Meanwhile, Nic's life and their children's lives continued to progress without her.

Camila's life wasn't just filled with loneliness and remorse. She was still a beautiful woman, and men often hit on her. She had several short-term flings, but none turned into long-term relationships. In retrospect, she regretted the drugs, the partying, the affair. Yet, she couldn't get over how easily Nic had given up on her. She often wondered how she could have miscalculated so badly, thinking she was a twelve out of ten while he was only a six. It wasn't supposed to end this way.

The realization hit her hard, and she struggled to hold back tears. She had lost not just a husband, but also the illusion of her own superiority.

CHAPTER 2
REFLECTIONS OF A BROKEN HEART

Camila and Nic met during their college years, swept up in a whirlwind romance. Nic remembered the first time they met, the way her eyes sparkled with excitement and curiosity. They bonded over their shared love for music and dancing, spending countless nights lost in the rhythms of merengue, salsa, and bachata. Those moments felt magical, as if the world outside ceased to exist when they were together. They laughed, dreamed, and planned a future that seemed so certain, so full of promise. Both young and ambitious, they shared dreams of success and a fulfilling life together.

Nic, a finance major, had a charismatic aura that drew Camila in. He was charming and confident, traits that captivated her. Camila, who was studying communication, found herself increasingly enchanted by him. Their love blossomed during late-night study sessions, coffee dates, and laughter echoing through campus halls.

They married shortly after graduation, driven by the excitement of their new lives and the belief that they would always prioritize each other. However, as the years passed, the vibrancy of their initial love began to fade. They settled into a routine that gradually became mundane. Nic's career took off, and he devoted himself to his work and his family with relentless determination.

Now, sitting on the porch, the Virginia sunset casting long shadows across the lawn, Nic found the tranquility of the suburbs a stark contrast to the bustling energy of New York City. He closed his eyes, memories of their college days flooding back. Watching his children play in the yard brought him immense joy and a hard-earned sense of peace. As he sipped his coffee, his mind wandered back to the early days with Camila.

Nic sat in the stillness of his home, his mind a whirlwind of confusion and heartache. Why would she do this to me? Wasn't I a good husband and provider? Memories of their life together flooded his thoughts, each one a painful reminder of the sweet girl he had met in college. That girl seemed like a distant memory now, replaced by a stranger who had shattered his trust. There were no answers, only a deep, gnawing bitterness and an overwhelming sense of loss.

He could still see her, twirling under the city lights, her laughter ringing in his ears. They had believed their chemistry would carry them to a happily ever after, but now that belief felt like a cruel joke. The vibrant, passionate woman he had fallen in love with had become a distant memory, overshadowed by betrayal. The silence of the house was deafening; each tick of the clock a reminder of the time that had slipped away. The life they had built together had been crumbling, and he had been powerless to stop it. All that remained were memories of what once was and the painful reality of what had become.

He remembered their wedding day, the promises they made, and the hope that filled their hearts. Moving to Virginia had seemed like the perfect start to their new life together. But as the years passed, cracks in their relationship began to show. Camila's restlessness and dissatisfaction with suburban life became more apparent. Nic tried to understand her, to support her, but nothing could quell her desire for excitement. The drinking, the drugs, the late-night parties—it all took a toll on their family.

His heart ached thinking about the nights he stayed up waiting for Camila to come home. He had taken on the role of both mother and father, trying to provide stability for their children amidst the chaos. He remembered the arguments, the tears, and the moment he realized he couldn't save their marriage. The decision to divorce had been one of the hardest things he had ever done. He loved Camila, but he knew that staying together was no longer healthy for any of them. As a single dad, he faced countless challenges but also discovered a strength he didn't know he possessed. His children became his anchor, their well-being his top priority.

Meeting Celia had been an unexpected blessing. She brought light and love back into his life, showing him that it was possible to find happiness again. Celia's kindness and understanding helped him heal, and together they built a new life filled with joy and mutual respect.

Yet, despite the happiness he had found, a part of Nic still felt a pang of sadness when he thought about Camila. He knew she struggled with regret and the consequences of her choices. He wished things could have been different, that she could have found the peace and fulfillment she sought.

His thoughts were interrupted by his daughter, Celina, who ran up to him with a beaming smile. "Dad, come play with us!" she exclaimed, pulling him towards the yard. He set his coffee down and followed her, his heart swelling with love and gratitude.

As he joined his children in their game, Nic realized that life had a way of moving forward, even when the past lingered in the background. He had learned to cherish the present, to appreciate the simple moments of joy and connection. While he couldn't change what had happened with Camila, he could continue to build a life filled with love and hope for the future.

Late at night, Nic sat on the edge of his bed, the room dimly lit and the house quiet. He held a photo of his family, reflecting on his past with Camila, his struggle with sobriety, his journey as a single dad, and the new life he was building with Celia. How did we get here? he wondered. I thought we had it all—a beautiful family, a happy home. But somewhere along the way, we lost each other.

The first five years of their marriage were far from perfect. Camila struggled with suburban life, which Nic thought was depression. Nic's drinking also affected their relationship and may have contributed to Camila's attitude. She wasn't always as present or helpful with the children or household duties as Nic would have liked. Yet, they both had their challenges and pushed through, trying to make a good life for their children. They fell into a routine of work, taking care of the home, and shuttling the kids to daycare. Some days were better organized and smoother than others, but each day presented its own challenges. They dealt with early morning rushes, forgotten school projects, last-minute grocery runs, and the constant balancing act of work and family life. Although it wasn't perfect, they had many good days, creating memories that made the relationship worth fighting for.

His thoughts drifted to happier times. He remembered a family picnic in the park—Camila laughing, the kids playing, and a pang of nostalgia hit him. He also recalled family game nights, some of their best moments together. The living room would transform into a lively battleground of laughter and playful banter. Adrián and Celina loved board games, their competitive spirit lighting up the room. Camila would tease him whenever he was on the brink of losing, and he would playfully groan in mock defeat.

"Come on, Dad, you can't let Celina win again!" Adrián would cheer, causing everyone to burst into laughter.

Those evenings were filled with camaraderie and joy, a stark contrast to the struggles that later ensued. Nic cherished the warmth of those moments, the way they bonded over silly games, and the genuine happiness radiating from his children's faces. They were all united as a family, without the clouds of regret and separation hanging over them.

I should have seen the signs he thought. Camila was slipping away, and I was too busy with work, too focused on providing, to notice. The fog of alcohol clouded his judgment, blurring the lines between reality and his desperate attempts to escape the mounting stress. Each drink numbed the pain temporarily but dulled his awareness. Nights spent in a haze, oblivious to the growing distance between them. Now that he was sober, he could clearly see how his alcoholism had affected his behavior, decisions, and judgment. Maybe if I had been more present, more attentive, things would have been different, he sighed, the weight of his regret heavy on his chest.

Feeling overwhelmed by his regrets, Nic put the kids to bed and then reached for his phone to call his friend Mike.

"Hey, Mike," Nic said, trying to keep his voice steady.

"Nic! How's it going?" Mike replied cheerfully.

"I'm hanging in there," Nic said, though the strain was clear in his tone.

Mike picked up on it immediately. "You sound down, man. Everything okay?"

Nic sighed, running a hand through his hair. "I don't know, Mike. I keep thinking about Camila and the kids. I feel like I failed them with my drinking. Camila made mistakes, but I can't put all the blame on her. I'm not excusing her behavior, just acknowledging how we got here."

Mike paused, then said, "You know, when I went through my rough patch, I kept beating myself up too. But sometimes, no matter how much you try, things just fall apart."

Nic managed a small smile. "Yeah, I guess. But I could have done more. I could have been there for her, helped her through her struggles. Instead, I let her drift away."

Mike chuckled softly. "Remember that time we tried to fix my old car? We did everything by the book, but it still broke down. Some things are just out of our control, man."

Nic sighed, the tension easing slightly. "Maybe you're right. But the guilt is still there, gnawing at me. I see the pain in Adrián and Celina's eyes, and I wonder if I could have prevented it."

Mike's tone softened. "You did your best, Nic. And look at you now sober, raising two great kids. That's something to be proud of."

"Thanks, man, I needed that pick-me-up, Nic replied. I need to remember how far we've come. I'm grateful for all the blessings in my life now—for my kids, for Celia, for friends like you. I've got a lot to be thankful for."

In a reflective moment, Nic sat with his mother, Victoria, in the living room. She was knitting, and he stared into the fireplace, lost in thought. "You're thinking about Camila again, aren't you?" Victoria asked softly.

"Yeah. I just can't shake the feeling that I could have done more," Nic whispered.

Victoria set her knitting aside. "We all have regrets, Nic. But you did what you thought was best for your family. You can't carry all the blame. It takes two to tango."

Nic sighed, his shoulders slumping. "I know, but it's hard. I see the kids struggling, and I feel responsible."

Victoria placed a comforting hand on his. "You gave her many chances, all of which she squandered. Remember what I told you the third time? A leopard never changes its spots. Expecting Camila to change was not realistic."

Nic nodded slowly. "I know, but the guilt... it's always there, a reminder of what could have been."

"The best thing you did for your family was to get sober. You kept your promise, hoping it would save your marriage and keep your family intact. Although Camila did not appreciate it, getting sober was the best thing you did for your children. They depended on you, and now, you just have to be there for them. Show them that life goes on and that they are loved."

Nic took a deep breath, feeling the weight of his responsibilities but also the support of his family and friends. "You're right, Mama. I need to focus on the present and be the best father I can be. The guilt will always be there, but I can't let it overshadow what's most important now—my children."

He hugged Victoria, grateful for her unwavering support. As he pulled away, he felt a renewed sense of purpose.

Nic's journey as a single dad was about providing stability for his children and building a new life with Celia. Through his healing process, he learned to balance his past and future, striving to be the best father while moving forward with hope and determination. He felt grateful for the blessings in his life—for his kids, for Celia, and for his supportive family and friends. Despite the challenges, he realized he had a lot to be thankful for.

Nic struggled with alcoholism, a genetic predisposition inherited from his mother's side of the family. Even one or two drinks could cause him to black out. He knew he had to get sober for his children's sake.

Nic's road to sobriety was tumultuous, marked by physical agony and emotional upheaval. Sitting on the edge of his bed, drenched in sweat, his hands trembled as he reached for a glass of water. The physical pain was excruciating, but the emotional turmoil was worse. Memories of past mistakes haunted him, and the urge to drink was overwhelming. He knew he had to fight through this for Adrián and Celina.

The initial hours brought anxiety and irritability. Despite his discomfort, Nic had to prepare breakfast for his children. Making toast and pouring cereal felt monumental. His hands shook as he packed their lunches and got them ready for school, forcing a smile to hide his pain.

As the hours dragged on, Nic experienced waves of intense sweating and chills. Hallucinations crept in—shadows moving in the corners of his vision, whispers that weren't there. He felt like he was losing his grip on reality, with the fear of seizures looming over him.

Despite the torment, Nic had to work. He couldn't afford to take time off, so he requested permission to work from home a few days a week. He struggled to focus, his mind clouded by pain and anxiety. Every task took twice as long, and he feared his colleagues would notice his trembling hands and pallor. Still he pushed through, knowing his children depended on his income.

The peak of his withdrawal brought the most intense symptoms. Nic's body ached, and his head throbbed with a relentless headache. Nausea made it hard to keep anything down, even water. He felt trapped in his own body, battling both physical pain and emotional despair. But amidst the chaos, there was a glimmer of hope. Nic reminded himself why he was enduring this torment. He pictured Adrián and Celina's faces, their smiles, and the life he wanted to build for them. Every moment of suffering was a step towards a better future, a future where he could be the father they deserved.

By the end of the first week, the most acute symptoms began to subside. Nic started to feel a bit more stable. Although he was still plagued by insomnia and mood swings, the physical pain lessened. However, the emotional challenges remained. The thought of his children's future was what kept him going.

Balancing work, household chores, and parenting continued to be a struggle, but Nic found small moments of joy in his children's laughter, trust, and reliance on him.

Even as the worst of the withdrawal symptoms faded, Nic knew he had a long road ahead. He continued to experience bouts of anxiety and mood swings but remained determined to stay sober. Seeking support from friends, family, and support groups, he learned new ways to cope with stress and triggers. Each day was a step toward rebuilding his life to give his family a better future.

Nic's journey to sobriety was fueled by an unwavering sense of responsibility and love for his family. He reminded himself of the little faces that looked up to him with trust and hope. Sobriety wasn't just a choice for Nic; it was a necessity. This immense responsibility gave him the courage to endure the physical and emotional pain of withdrawal. He knew that every step towards sobriety was a step towards a better future for his family. Nic's love for Adrián and Celina became his guiding light.

Nic faced myriad emotional challenges during his journey to sobriety. He was haunted by memories of his past mistakes. The guilt of not being there for his children and the shame of his actions weighed heavily on him, often intensifying his cravings for alcohol as a way to numb the pain.

Without a supportive wife, Nic often felt isolated. The absence of a partner to share the burden of parenting and recovery made him feel incredibly lonely, sometimes making the emotional pain even more acute. Everyday stressors could act as triggers, and Nic had to learn new ways to cope with them without turning to alcohol. He had to develop new strategies to deal with anger, frustration, and sadness in a healthy way.

Despite these challenges, Nic's love for Adrián and Celina gave him the strength to persevere. He knew that overcoming these emotional hurdles was essential for his sobriety and the future of his family.

Freed from the fog of alcohol, Nic embraced a healthier lifestyle, working out regularly and undergoing a striking physical transformation. He looked healthier and more vibrant, with increased energy levels. He started taking better care of himself, and his children noticed the change, feeling a sense of pride in their father's progress. With his improved health came newfound emotional stability. Nic became more patient and understanding. The home, once filled with tension and uncertainty, transformed into a place of calm and stability. Adrián and Celina began to feel more secure and loved.

Nic engaged in activities his children enjoyed. They played sports together, cooked meals, and had family game nights. These shared moments brought laughter and joy back into their lives. Celina, in particular, loved baking cookies with her dad, their laughter filling the kitchen.

Nic often struggled with the temptation to drink. While his home was a safe haven free from alcohol, attending social events where alcohol was everywhere proved much more difficult. One evening, at a company-sponsored event, he felt the familiar urge. Remembering the promise he made to himself, he stepped outside to get some fresh air and called Adrián, just to check in. His son's voice encouraged him to stay strong, and Nic overcame the challenge.

Nic achieved personal goals, like earning a promotion at work and completing a marathon. These accomplishments strengthened his relationship with his children, showing them the power of perseverance and dedication.

His relationship with Celia became a cornerstone of his new life. They shared a deep connection built on trust and mutual respect. Celia understood his past and supported his journey to sobriety without judgment. She encouraged him to embrace a healthier lifestyle, joining him in his workouts and even running alongside him in the marathon. Their partnership became a source of strength for Nic, providing the love and stability he had once thought lost.

One evening, after putting the kids to bed, Nic and Celia sat on the porch, enjoying the cool night air. "I'm proud of you, Nic," Celia said, her eyes reflecting her sincerity. "You've come such a long way, and you're an amazing father."

Nic smiled, feeling a warmth spread through him. "I couldn't have done it without you, Celia. You've been my rock."

Celia took his hand, squeezing it gently. "We're in this together. The kids and I are lucky to have you."

As they sat in comfortable silence, Nic reflected on his journey. Through challenges and triumphs, and with the support of his children, Celia, and his own determination, he had built a life filled with love and hope. Grateful for this second chance, he was committed to making the most of it.

Nic's life was now a testament to the power of resilience and the strength of the human spirit. Through his struggles and triumphs, he had created a new chapter for himself and his family—one marked by healing, growth, and unwavering love.

CHAPTER 3

RHYTHMS OF NEW YORK CITY: CAMILA'S ROOTS

Camila Castillo was born on April 21, 1980, in the heart of New York City's Dominican community, a neighborhood teeming with life and culture. Her family, first-generation immigrants from the Dominican Republic, settled in a close-knit community where everyone knew each other. The streets were alive with the sounds of merengue, salsa, and bachata, while the aroma of traditional Dominican dishes wafted through the air, creating a sense of home away from home.

Immigrants in the US often choose to live in communities with others from their native countries for a sense of security while adapting to a new culture and language. This familiarity provides comfort, but the adaptation process is still challenging. They must navigate educational and psychosocial difficulties as they learn a new language and integrate into a new community, balancing two worlds—conducting business in English while maintaining their native language and customs with family and friends.

Camila's family was her anchor. Her hardworking and resilient parents instilled in her the importance of family, respect, and perseverance. Large family gatherings were a staple, where laughter and stories flowed as freely as the food. These gatherings celebrated their cultural heritage, alive with the colors and flavors of the Dominican Republic.

Music and dance were the heartbeat of these gatherings. The living room transformed into a dance floor, with her parents leading the way, their movements fluid and joyful, embodying the spirit of their homeland. While the adults danced to traditional music, the children dashed in and out of the apartment, up and down the hallway and stairs, darting to the corner store to buy candy.

The music was loud, the conversations louder, and the happiness palpable. It was astounding how many people packed into those apartments. Despite the lively activities, no one ever complained about the music, the children's antics, or the boisterous conversations that lasted into the early morning hours.

During one such gathering, the living room swirled with color and sound. Camila's mother, Andrea, stirred a pot of sancocho, its rich aroma filling the apartment. Camila, ten at the time, danced around with her younger sisters, their laughter mingling with the upbeat rhythms of merengue.

"Camila, come help me set the table," Andrea called out. Camila spun around, her dress flaring, and skipped to the kitchen.

"Sure, Mami," she said, grabbing the plates. "Do you think Tio Juan will tell his funny stories again?"

Andrea smiled, her eyes twinkling. "He always does. Now, make sure you put the forks on the left."

As the family gathered around the table, the room buzzed with conversation and laughter. Camila's father, Carlos, raised his glass. "To family," he said, his voice strong and warm. "And to the dreams we build together."

Living in a bustling New York City neighborhood, Camila was surrounded by diversity. Her community was a mosaic of cultures, each contributing to the vibrant tapestry of her upbringing. The local bodegas, with their colorful displays of tropical fruits and spices, served as a daily reminder of her roots. The neighborhood was more than just a place to live; it was a support network where neighbors looked out for each other, creating a sense of belonging and security. On weekends, the neighborhood would come alive with impromptu dance parties, where neighbors gathered to celebrate life's joys and forget its hardships, if only for a while.

Camila's childhood in New York City was a blend of cultural richness and personal challenges, shaping her into the strong, determined woman she would become. Her story exemplified resilience, cultural pride, and the enduring spirit of a first-generation American striving to honor her roots while forging her own path.

Camila was striking, standing at 5'7" with dark, flowing hair cascading down her back. Her fair skin had an ethereal glow, accentuating her symmetrical features. Her piercing brown eyes captivated anyone who met her gaze.

Her high cheekbones and full lips added to her allure, giving her a timeless elegance. Camila's slender neck and graceful posture exuded confidence, commanding attention in any room she entered. She carried herself with a poise that bordered on arrogance, aware of the power her beauty held.

Her curvaceous figure complemented her striking appearance. Yet, this outer perfection masked inner turmoil and moral decay—an ugliness that became apparent to those who got to know her. Despite her captivating presence, Camila's true nature was marred by her tendency to manipulate situations and people to her advantage, revealing a complex and flawed character beneath the surface.

Camila's parents, practical and well-grounded, placed a high value on education, seeing it as the key to a better future. They often reminded her that beauty fades, but knowledge endures. Andrea was adamant that her daughters be financially independent, never relying on a man for support. She often said, "Stay with a man because you want to, not because you need to."

Encouraged to excel in school, Camila thrived, driven by a desire to honor her parents' sacrifices. Despite the obstacles, she dreamed of achieving more than what her immediate environment offered. Her aspirations were fueled by a determination to make a name for herself, creating a life that reflected both her Dominican heritage and her American dreams.

The challenges of being a first-generation American instilled in Camila a sense of resilience and determination. These traits would later prove crucial as she navigated the complexities of her marriage and personal life. Despite the struggles, she maintained a deep pride in her Dominican heritage, which influenced her values, traditions, and the way she envisioned raising her own family.

In high school, Camila was the queen bee, effortlessly popular and always at the center of attention. She excelled in social settings but often neglected her studies, relying on her charm to get by.

"Hey, Camila," a boy named Alex called out as she walked down the hallway. "Need help with that history paper?"

Camila flashed him a dazzling smile. "That would be great, Alex. You're a lifesaver."

As Alex walked away, her friend Sofia nudged her. "You know, you could do it yourself if you tried."

Camila shrugged. "Why bother when I don't have to?"

The transition from Camila's childhood to her college years brought both excitement and anxiety. She attended Pace University on a full academic scholarship, choosing Communication as her major—a field she believed required minimal effort. She focused heavily on her social life, dating several high-profile individuals and ensuring she was seen with the right people. Her relationships were often superficial; she preferred admiration and envy over genuine intimacy, which made forming deep connections difficult.

Camila's beauty and charm opened doors to exclusive parties and influential circles, reinforcing her belief that her looks were her most valuable asset. But beneath the surface, she grappled with deep insecurities. The pressure to succeed academically and professionally weighed heavily on her, knowing her parents had sacrificed so much for her future.

As a first-generation American, Camila faced unique challenges in navigating her Dominican heritage and American culture. The pressure to succeed was constant, especially during her teenage years, when peer pressure and societal expectations clashed with her cultural values.

During these times, music became her solace. The emotive storytelling of bachata resonated deeply with her, its themes of love, heartbreak, and longing always captivated her. Dancing became a way for her to process her emotions and feel connected to something larger than herself. In the quiet of the night, she would lie awake, listening to the sounds of the city outside her window, wondering if she could ever truly balance her Dominican heritage with her American dreams.

Born in the U.S., she constantly balanced American culture with her Dominican roots. Despite a supportive community, navigating these two worlds was arduous. She had to honor her parents' traditions while searching for her own identity, trying not to compromise the values of the old world. Each day was a delicate dance between cultures as she strove to forge a new path without losing herself. In the end, she often wondered which culture would ultimately shape her life and personality, questioning whether she could blend both worlds or if one would dominate her future.

Navigating life as a person from mixed cultures is a journey of evolving into something uniquely your own. You're not just a blend of two cultures; you become a new entity, often not fully accepted by either side because you don't fit neatly into their definitions. This in-betweenness can be isolating yet beautiful, creating a unique identity that embodies elements of both worlds while transcending them. It's an experience that forges a path entirely your own, reflecting a rich tapestry of diverse experiences and perspectives. It's about finding strength in the spaces between and creating a new narrative that is both personal and a testament to the cultures that shaped you.

CHAPTER 4

FULL CIRCLE: NIC'S JOURNEY FROM NEW YORK TO VIRGINIA

Nicolas (Nic) Garcia was born on August 20, 1980, in Manhattan's Upper West Side, to Dominican immigrants who had themselves grown up in New York since the age of six. This unique blend of cultures shaped Nic's upbringing into a mix of Dominican traditions and American influences. His parents, having spent most of their lives in New York, were more Americanized than other immigrant families yet held onto their Dominican roots with pride.

When Nic was ten years old, his father's job relocated the family to Fairfax, Virginia. The move marked a dramatic shift from the bustling streets of Manhattan to the quieter, suburban life of Fairfax. Nic stood in the middle of their new, spacious living room, feeling the silence press in on him. The absence of honking taxis, police sirens, and the distant hum of the city made him feel as though he were on another planet.

"Nic, come help unpack your room," his mother called from upstairs. He trudged up the stairs, each step feeling heavier than the last. His room was filled with boxes, but it was the framed photo of his friends from New York that caught his eye. He picked it up, a pang of homesickness hitting him hard.

"Do you miss it already?" his father asked, leaning against the doorframe.

Nic nodded, unable to find the words to express the turmoil inside him. "Yeah, I do."

Although he missed his friends and New York, Fairfax offered its own advantages. Nic and his brothers delighted in running up and down the stairs, sliding on the banister, and exploring their spacious house. This was a welcome change from their two-bedroom apartment in New York, where they had shared a bedroom. In Fairfax, they each had their own room, and Nic cherished the privacy.

Their home remained a vibrant hub of Dominican culture, despite the geographical shift. The sounds of merengue, salsa, and bachata filled their house, and family gatherings overflowed with laughter, music, and the rich aromas of traditional Dominican cuisine. These gatherings became Nic's lifeline to his roots. His parents danced to the lively beats of Wilfrido Vargas, his mom often pulling him into the dance. "Remember, mijo," she'd say, "no matter where we are, our culture is in our hearts."

Nic's parents believed that moving to the suburbs meant escaping the dangers of inner-city life. In New York, they knew what to look for and how to recognize trouble. But in the affluent, manicured lawns of Fairfax, they assumed the risks were minimal. The polite, articulate kids with good grades and well-dressed appearances masked a different reality. On weekends, empty houses and hotels transformed into wild party venues with drugs and alcohol. Nic's parents soon realized that suburban kids were just as susceptible to high-risk behaviors as their inner-city counterparts, if not more so.

The family often traveled back to New York for holidays and special occasions. During the four-hour drive, his parents always had music playing. As a child, Nic loved these trips, where he and his brothers could run around freely while the adults talked and danced. He'd ask the adults for money to go to the store, and after a few drinks, no one ever refused. Nic capitalized on their generosity, buying as much candy and junk food as he could.

In Fairfax, music took on even greater significance for Nic. It served as both a link to his past and a source of comfort in his new environment. His parents continued to play their favorite Dominican tunes, and family gatherings always featured dancing and singing. These moments celebrated their culture, keeping their traditions alive despite the distance from their homeland. Nic learned merengue, salsa, and bachata at a young age, guided by his parents' enthusiastic instruction. These dances represented more than just movements; they were expressions of identity and emotion. The rhythms resonated with him deeply, providing a sense of belonging and continuity.

Growing up in Fairfax, Nic often felt pulled between two worlds. At school, he was immersed in American culture, while at home, his parents ensured he maintained his Dominican heritage. This duality sometimes made him feel as though he were living two separate lives, striving to fit in with his peers while honoring his family's traditions. Yet he navigated these challenges with resilience, successfully blending the best of both cultures.

One day, as Nic sat alone in the cafeteria, he picked at his lunch and watched his classmates laughing and chatting. He felt a pang of isolation, still getting to know everyone. As he took in the boisterous scene, a group of boys approached him.

"Hey, Nic, why don't you ever hang out with us?" one of them asked.

Nic shrugged, trying to hide his discomfort. "I don't know. Just busy, I guess."

The boy smiled. "Well, you should join us sometime. We're playing basketball after school."

Nic's face lit up. "Yeah, maybe I will."

Soon, Nic joined the football team and played throughout elementary and high school. During his junior year, his team won the state championship, an exhilarating experience. He loved the camaraderie of the team. Playing football helped him develop discipline and teamwork, shaping him and instilling values of perseverance and commitment. Nic excelled both academically and socially, balancing his school life with his rich cultural heritage. He embraced his dual identity, thriving in both worlds.

Nic's parents emphasized the importance of education, believing it was the key to success. They encouraged him to pursue his dreams and supported his academic endeavors. Nic excelled in school, driven by a desire to make his parents proud and to create a future that honored their sacrifices. His hard work paid off when he was accepted into Pace University in New York. Returning to New York for college felt like coming full circle.

He embraced the city's energy anew, immersing himself in his studies and the diverse cultural experiences that Pace University offered.

CHAPTER 5

FROM COLLEGE DREAMS TO BROKEN VOWS

In the first week of her sophomore year, Camila collided with Nic in the bustling campus courtyard, sending coffee splashing across his books. "Oh my God, I'm so sorry!" she exclaimed.

Nic looked up, his initial annoyance melting into a smile. "No worries. I'm Nic, by the way."

"I'm Camila. Let me help you with that," she replied, flustered but intrigued. As they gathered his books, their hands brushed, and a spark of connection ignited between them.

"How about I replace that cup of coffee?" Nic offered. What started as a quick cup of coffee into a two-hour conversation. They exchanged contact information and promised to meet again, marking the beginning of their compelling relationship.

Late-night study sessions evolved into deep conversations about life, dreams, and fears. They explored the city together, discovering hidden cafes and bustling parks. One evening, under the twinkling lights of a small bistro, Nic took Camila's hand. "I know it's crazy, but I feel like I've known you forever," he said softly.

Camila's eyes sparkled. "Me too." Their first kiss that night was a promise of a future they both believed in. Dancing became the cornerstone of their relationship.

As graduation approached, their conversations grew serious. Nic felt drawn to Virginia, the familiarity of his hometown calling to him. Camila, however, was enchanted by the possibilities of New York.

One night, the tension between their dreams came to a head. "Camila, I know New York is your home, but have you considered what life would be like for us in the city? Raising kids in the city is challenging. The cost of living is sky-high, and we'd be constantly worried about money," Nic said.

Camila's eyes filled with tears. "But New York is where I feel alive, Nic. I can't imagine leaving it behind."

Nic reached for her hand, his voice softening. "I understand that but think about the future. In Virginia, we can afford a nice house with a yard. Our kids can play outside, and we won't be crammed into a tiny apartment. The schools are excellent, and it's a safer environment. We'll have more time for each other, less time commuting and worrying about making ends meet."

Camila looked away, her heart torn. "I just... I don't know if I can give up the city. It's all I've ever known."

Nic gently turned her face back to his. "I know it's a big change, but we can build a beautiful life there. We can still visit New York whenever we want. It doesn't have to be all or nothing."

She sighed, the weight of the decision pressing down on her. "I just need some time to think about it."

Nic nodded. "Take all the time you need. Just know that whatever we decide, we'll face it together."

As days passed, Camila's thoughts swirled. She weighed the hustle and charm of New York against the promise of a calmer life in Virginia. One evening, as she gazed out at the city skyline, she felt a quiet resolve. She loved Nic deeply, and more than the city itself, she loved the future they could build together. The Big Apple might always hold a piece of her heart, but a life filled with love and potential awaited in Virginia.

Nic and Camila's relationship blossomed over two years of dating as they met each other's families and explored the city with friends and family. Their love and bond grew stronger, and they began discussing a future together. They often made weekend trips to Virginia, where Nic's family lived, and Camila's family in New York City embraced Nic immediately, loving him as one of their own. On weekends, they found Latin dance clubs in the city, losing themselves in the rhythms of merengue, salsa, and bachata. The music bridged their past and present, celebrating their shared heritage.

Camila finally came to her decision, turning to Nic with a mixture of determination and peace in her eyes. "Alright, let's do this. Let's build that beautiful life together."

Nic's face lit up as he wrapped her in an embrace, knowing they were

about to embark on a wonderful journey, side by side. They married immediately after graduating from Pace University in 2002.

On June 29, 2002, Nic and Camila exchanged vows in an intimate ceremony in New York City, surrounded by close friends and family. The heartfelt vows and beautiful exchange of rings took place under a canopy of twinkling fairy lights in a charming garden setting. As they promised each other a lifetime of love, the air was filled with the sweet scent of blooming flowers and soft music played by a string quartet.

After the ceremony, they moved to a cozy reception where the room was filled with laughter, love, and memorable toasts. Friends and family shared stories and well-wishes, creating a warm and joyful atmosphere. The couple's first dance was to their favorite Latin song, blending their shared heritage with their love story. The evening ended with everyone dancing under the stars, a perfect blend of simplicity and charm to mark the beginning of their journey together.

For their honeymoon, Nic and Camila escaped to the sun-kissed beaches of Punta Cana, Dominican Republic. They spent their days basking in the tropical sun, exploring the vibrant culture, and dancing to the rhythms of the Caribbean. The breathtaking sunsets, serene ocean waves, and romantic evenings by the beach made their honeymoon unforgettable. It was a beautiful and peaceful interlude before they made their final move to Virginia to start their new life together.

As they drove from New York to Virginia, Camila sat in the passenger seat, watching the cityscape fade into the distance. The excitement and energy of the city had always been her lifeline, a source of inspiration and vitality. As the familiar skyline disappeared, a sense of loss settled over her. She glanced at Nic, who focused on the road, his expression a mix of determination and hope. He had always been her rock, the steady presence in her life, but now she felt an unfamiliar distance between them.

Why am I doing this? she wondered, her heart heavy with doubt. The decision to move to Virginia had been made out of love, a compromise she hoped would bring them closer. But as the miles stretched on, she couldn't shake the feeling that she was leaving a part of herself behind.

Camila's thoughts drifted to their life in New York as college students: the late-night dance sessions, spontaneous adventures, and vibrant culture that always made her feel alive. She had thrived in the city's chaos, finding joy in its unpredictability. Now, as they drove to Virginia, with her belongings packed in the car, she projected an image of quiet suburbs and a slower pace, which felt like a foreign land. She worried about losing her sense of self and becoming someone she didn't recognize.

Sitting in the car with Nic, Camila felt a wave of doubt wash over her. She began to admit to herself that she might not have been ready for marriage and everything that came with it. The idea of settling down and embracing the roles of wife and mother felt suffocating. Motherhood had always been a distant concept to her, something she admired in others but never truly envisioned for herself. She loved Nic deeply, but the thought of giving up the only life she knew in New York for a life she wasn't sure she wanted filled her with anxiety.

As they crossed state lines, Camila tried to focus on the positives. She reminded herself of the love they shared, the dreams in which they had once believed. But the nagging doubts persisted, a constant reminder of the sacrifices she was making. She glanced at Nic again, his profile illuminated by the setting sun. He looked so hopeful, so certain that this move would be the start of something beautiful.

Maybe I'm just being paranoid, she thought, trying to reassure herself. I hope he's right, she thought, a tear slipping down her cheek. I hope I can find happiness here, for both our sakes.

During the first year of their marriage, Camila became pregnant. Both she and Nic were thrilled. However, Camila soon struggled with withdrawal symptoms and depression due to her inability to drink alcohol. Although she didn't consider herself an alcoholic, she resented not being able to go out, party, and drink. For many women, pregnancy is an awe-inspiring experience filled with anticipation, joy, and wonder. But Camila hated being pregnant. It cramped her style; she was gaining weight, and her ankles were swollen.

Finally, after nine long months, Adrián was born on September 21, 2003, weighing 8 pounds. Nic was present during the delivery and in awe of the process. He was excited to take his baby boy home. Camila, however, remained indifferent. She did not appreciate the crying, lack of sleep, and resented all the attention the baby required. Consequently, Nic assumed the roles of both mother and father for Adrián.

Nic cradled Adrián in his arms, marveling at the tiny fingers and toes. "Look at him, Camila," he said, his voice filled with wonder. "He's perfect." Camila glanced at the baby, her expression unreadable. "Yeah, he's cute," she replied, her tone flat. Nic's heart sank. He had hoped that holding their son would spark some maternal instinct in her, but Camila remained distant, almost detached.

As the weeks passed, Nic found himself taking on more responsibilities. He changed diapers, rocked Adrián to sleep, and sang lullabies in the middle of the night. One evening, as he was preparing a bottle, he noticed Camila sitting on the couch, scrolling through her phone.

"Camila, can you hold him for a minute?" he asked, trying to keep the frustration out of his voice.

She sighed, barely looking up. "I'm really tired, Nic. Can't you do it?"

Nic clenched his jaw, the weight of his new role pressing down on him. "Sure, I'll take care of it," he said, forcing a smile.

Camila sat on the couch, her phone a welcome distraction from the overwhelming reality of motherhood. She glanced at Nic, who was busy preparing a bottle for Adrián. She felt a pang of guilt but quickly pushed it aside. This wasn't the life she had envisioned for herself. The constant crying, the sleepless nights, the endless cycle of feeding and changing—it all felt suffocating.

She missed the freedom of her old life, the spontaneous nights out, the thrill of the city. Motherhood had stripped her of her identity, leaving her feeling trapped and resentful. She loved Adrián deeply, but the demands of taking care of him were overwhelming. She couldn't wait for Nic to get home or to drop Adrián at the sitter just to breathe. Although she adored her son, she couldn't shake the feeling that she was losing herself.

One night, after a particularly rough day, Camila found herself at a party, drink in hand. The music was loud, the lights dim, and for a moment, she felt like her old self again. But as the night wore on, the emptiness returned, gnawing at her insides. She stumbled home, disheveled and intoxicated, to find Nic waiting for her, worry etched on his face.

"Where have you been?" he demanded, his voice tight with concern.

"Out," she replied defiantly. "I needed a break."

"We have a baby at home, Camila. You can't just disappear like that."

"I can't do this, Nic," she said, tears streaming down her face. "I feel like I'm drowning."

Nic's expression softened, but the hurt in his eyes was unmistakable. "I know it's hard, but we have to figure this out together. For Adrián."

The strain on their marriage became palpable. Nic tried to talk to Camila, to understand her feelings and find ways to help her adjust. But Camila grew more distant, her mind always elsewhere. She resented suburban life and felt suffocated by the responsibilities of marriage and motherhood.

As the years passed, the gap between Camila and Nic widened. Nic remained a steady presence in his family's lives, providing them with the stability and love they needed. Camila, however, drifted further away, caught in a cycle of self-destruction and regret.

By the third year of their marriage, Camila's second pregnancy, though unplanned, brought both joy and looming fears. Both she and Nic were thrilled, but like the first, Camila struggled with feelings of resentment and depression. Everyone was aware of her challenges as a mother and couldn't believe they were having another child. Nic was overwhelmed with household chores—cooking, cleaning, laundry—all while holding down his job. He loved Camila deeply, hoping she would eventually find contentment, but her behavior grew more erratic, and Nic's hope began to wane.

Nic was present at the birth of their daughter, Celina, on April 20, 2006. She was a beautiful baby who resembled her mother, with fair skin and a head full of dark, straight hair. Nic held Celina close, her tiny body fitting perfectly in his arms. "She's beautiful, Camila," he whispered, tears of joy in his eyes. "Just like you."

Camila forced a smile, but her heart wasn't in it. The weight of her responsibilities felt heavier than ever. She watched Nic with their daughter, his face glowing with pride and love, and felt a pang of something she couldn't quite identify. Why couldn't she feel the same way?

Camila stared at Celina, her emotions a tangled mess. She wanted to love her daughter, to feel the same joy Nic did, but all she felt was numbness. The crying, sleepless nights, and constant demands—it was all too much. She longed for the freedom she once had, the life she had left behind.

One night, after another wild party, Camila came home late, disheveled and intoxicated. Nic was waiting for her, worry etched on his face. They argued, the tension that had been building for years finally erupting. Camila accused Nic of trying to control her, while Nic pleaded with her to think of their children and the life they had built.

The argument ended with Camila storming out, leaving Nic to pick up the pieces. He put the children to bed and sat alone in the quiet house, wondering where it had all gone wrong. He loved Camila, but he couldn't ignore the toll her actions were taking on their family.

Camila's search for excitement led her down a darker path. She continued to party and use drugs, distancing herself further from Nic and their children. The thrill she sought was always fleeting, leaving her feeling emptier and more lost than before.

From the outside, Camila and Nic's life seemed perfect—a beautiful home, successful careers, and a picture-perfect family. But inside, Camila's heart felt like a lead weight. The spark of their college romance had dimmed, and her feelings for Nic had withered. She wandered through their home, her eyes glazing over the family photos on the walls, searching for a happiness that seemed just out of reach.

Their married life had begun with joy. Nic, ever the devoted husband and father, juggled his demanding job with family time. He would come home exhausted but still managed to cook dinner, help with homework, and organize weekend picnics. To an outsider, their family appeared to be the epitome of perfection—a thoughtful husband, a caring wife, and two well-behaved children.

As the years passed, Camila's dissatisfaction with her marriage and life deepened. The stability that once comforted her now felt like a golden cage. She would sit at the kitchen table, staring at the same four walls, feeling an emptiness gnawing at her. She longed for something more intense, more passionate than the predictable rhythm of suburban life.

Seeking escape, Camila viewed Nic and their suburban existence as symbols of the monotony she despised. She started frequenting bars, indulging in alcohol and drugs, seeking the thrill of late-night parties. Nic, sensing the growing distance, took on more household duties, trying to shield their children from the turmoil.

Camila's physical and emotional presence at home became increasingly rare. Often lost in her phone, she was more engaged with her online persona than with her family. Nic and the children felt the void of her emotional absence. Despite the widening rift, Nic clung to the hope of reconciliation. He would sit in their bedroom, looking at old photos, his heart heavy with the weight of their disintegrating marriage. He fought for their relationship, believing that somehow, they could find their way back to each other. But each day, the erosion of their bond felt more like an inevitable collapse.

CHAPTER 6
BETRAYAL IN THE SHADOWS

Nic, the diligent finance manager, spent most of his days in spreadsheets, providing a comfortable life for his wife and their two children. Camila, in contrast, was vibrant and outgoing, often the life of neighborhood gatherings. Many saw them as a perfect balance—Nic's quiet stability complementing Camila's spirited personality. However, the cracks beneath the surface remained invisible to outsiders.

Tension had been mounting. Nic was stretched thin, juggling long hours at work with household responsibilities. He managed the cooking, cleaning, and children's needs while maintaining his job. Despite his efforts, he often found himself absent both physically and emotionally. Camila, instead of appreciating his dedication, felt neglected. She yearned for excitement and attention, interpreting Nic's constant busyness as indifference. Their communication deteriorated, and soon, Camila's boredom with domestic life led her down dangerous paths. She craved excitement, desperate to break free from the monotony that had consumed her life.

Raising children often feels like a whirlwind, with every moment revolving around their needs and schedules. Social lives take a backseat, and priorities shift dramatically. Late-night feedings, school drop-offs, and endless activities fill the days, leaving little room for anything else. Amidst the chaos lies a profound beauty in the selflessness that parenting brings forth. It's about finding joy in their milestones and watching them grow, knowing they are our world. In giving so much of ourselves, we discover the depths of our love and resilience.

But for Camila, this stage felt suffocating. She missed the freedom of her old life, the spontaneous nights out, the thrill of the city. Instead of finding joy in Adrián's milestones as he learned to read and explore the world with boundless energy at four years old, or Celina's first steps and babbling at one, she resented their constant demands. The sleepless nights, the endless cycle of feeding, changing, and managing tantrums—it all overwhelmed her. Watching Nic bond with the children while she felt distant only heightened her sense of isolation. She couldn't shake the feeling that she was losing herself.

Camila loved her children, but the selflessness of motherhood felt like a shackle. She watched other mothers embrace their roles, finding fulfillment in their children's happiness, and wondered why she couldn't feel the same. She hoped that when Adrián and Celina grew older and required less constant attention, she might feel more connected. But the resentment deepened, and she yearned for something more, something to reignite the spark she had lost.

Nic, consumed by work and fatherhood, remained unaware of the depth of her struggle. His long hours and constant busyness left little time for meaningful connection, leaving Camila feeling increasingly isolated and unappreciated. The gap between them widened, pushing her further into her feelings of loneliness and longing. Her search for excitement led her down paths that threatened to unravel everything they had built, as she sought to reclaim a sense of identity and purpose beyond the roles of wife and mother.

Camila appeared to be the perfect wife, but beneath the surface, things were unraveling. By their second year of marriage, the demands of motherhood, maintaining a home, and work had begun to strain their relationship. Camila grew increasingly lonely and frustrated. The tension between them became evident to their friends. The couple, once the life of every social gathering, withdrew. At events, Nic drank excessively while Camila appeared distant, absorbed in her phone.

As the years passed, Camila's dissatisfaction with her life intensified, exacerbating her careless, selfish, and irresponsible behavior. Lost in her search for something to fill the void, she increasingly neglected her family's needs, thinking only of herself. During this period of growing discontent, Camila embarked on an affair.

As the Director of Public Relations for her company, Camila had to attend various events. During a charity event her boss asked her to attend, she met Marcos Medina, a 38-year-old corporate lawyer.

Marcos leaned against the bar, scanning the room. It was a typical Friday night at the upscale lounge, filled with the murmur of conversation and the clinking of glasses. Then he saw her. Camila entered, commanding attention with her striking beauty, dark flowing hair, and ethereal presence. Marcos couldn't look away. She moved with grace and confidence, her eyes scanning the crowd for a familiar face. Their gazes met, and for a moment, the noise of the lounge faded away. Marcos felt an immediate, undeniable connection.

He moved closer, his heart pounding. "Hi," he said, his voice steady despite his nerves. "Can I buy you a drink?"

Camila turned to him, her eyes meeting his with curious intensity. "Sure," she replied, a small smile playing on her lips. "I'll have a glass of red wine."

As the bartender poured her drink, Marcos introduced himself. "I'm Marcos. I don't think I've seen you here before."

"I'm Camila," she said, taking a sip of her wine. "I don't usually attend these events, but my boss asked me to represent our firm and support the charity."

They fell into easy conversation, discussing everything from books to career aspirations. Marcos was captivated by her intelligence and wit, while his warmth and charm made Camila feel seen and appreciated in a way that had become rare with Nic. As the evening progressed, they shared stories about their work, demonstrating genuine interest in each other's thoughts. The hours slipped by until the lounge announced closing time.

As they walked into the cool night air, Marcos felt a surge of anticipation. Something about Camila drew him in inexplicably. They reached her car, and she turned to face him.

"Thank you for the drink and conversation," she said, her eyes searching his.

"Anytime," Marcos replied. "I'd love to see you again."

Camila smiled, a hint of sadness in her eyes. "Maybe," she said softly. "Goodnight, Marcos."

As she drove away, Marcos stood watching her taillights disappear into the night. Determined to see her again, he returned to the lounge to check the guest log. "Lucinda Martinez," he said aloud. He searched the room until he found Lucinda and asked her for Camila's contact information.

Camila's attraction to Marcos was immediate. He made her feel seen and desired. When he called, she felt a mixture of surprise and anticipation.

"Camila, how are you? This is Marcos, from the charity event."

"Of course I remember you, Marcos. I'm doing well, how are you?"

"Very well, thank you. I can't stop thinking about you since last Friday and want to see you again. Will you join me for a drink?"

Camila hesitated, knowing it was wrong. The temptation overwhelmed her, and she agreed, feeling neglected in her marriage.

Camila arranged with her company to attend various functions where she knew Marcos would be. During these events, they got better acquainted. Their conversations deepened, evolving from casual chats to late-night discussions about hopes, dreams, and life's frustrations. Camila confided in Marcos about her issues with Nic—the emotional distance, the neglect. Marcos, ever the smooth talker, validated her feelings, assuring her she deserved better. He offered a listening ear and supportive friendship, filling the void in her life. His attention felt like a breath of fresh air, replacing the emptiness Nic's emotional absence had created.

The emotional connection with Marcos blossomed into flirtation, igniting a spark Camila thought long extinguished. While Nic remained immersed in work, oblivious to the changes in his wife's life, Camila found herself at a crossroads. The love story she had cherished was overshadowed by loneliness and her need for validation. With each passing day, her bond with Marcos deepened, leading her further from the woman she once was and closer to the dangerous allure of an affair.

Initially rooted in friendship, their relationship flourished as Marcos listened to her marital frustrations with magnetic charm that made her feel valued—a stark contrast to Nic's growing indifference. Their conversations flowed effortlessly, often continuing long after their professional meetings ended. One evening, after a company event, Marcos invited her for drinks. They sat in a cozy bar with dim lighting, the atmosphere alive with laughter and clinking glasses. As they talked, Camila felt liberated in his presence. He made her laugh, teasing her about her worries and reminding her of long-forgotten joys. The tension of her day dissolved, replaced by an exhilarating connection. As they shared stories, she found herself drawing closer, captivated by the warmth in his gaze.

Their meetings were electric, the chemistry between them undeniable. Camila laughed and smiled in ways she hadn't in months. Initially light and flirtatious, their interactions evolved into confiding about personal struggles. Camila began finding excuses to see Marcos, who welcomed the attention. He found himself enchanted by Camila's vivacity, feeling alive in her presence. One night, after a few drinks, their first kiss ignited a fire within both of them. What started as innocent flirtation transformed into a full-blown passionate affair. Camila felt a rush of excitement she hadn't experienced in years.

They met in parks at night, hotel rooms during the day, and sometimes at Marcos's apartment. Each encounter deepened their bond as Camila became consumed by her desire for him. The thrill of the forbidden consumed them both. Marcos masterfully used his position of power to ensure no one suspected anything, while Camila struggled with mounting guilt. Despite the shame, the passion between them was undeniable.

As the affair intensified, so did the risk of discovery. For months, Camila and Marcos lived in a bubble of secrecy and passion. But as with all affairs, the tension of living a double life began to wear on them. Marcos became more possessive, often questioning Camila about her time with Nic. Camila felt torn between her loyalty to her husband and her overwhelming desire for Marcos.

Despite the thrill, Camila felt guilty. Betraying Nic was wrong. Their marriage wasn't perfect, but he was a good man who didn't deserve this. Still, the excitement and attention Marcos gave her proved too addictive to let go. As months passed, Camila's obsession with Marcos deepened. Her lies to Nic became more frequent, claiming she was at the gym or out with friends when she was meeting Marcos.

Marcos became her escape, her chance to live the passionate, exciting life she had always dreamed of but never thought possible. However, their relationship wasn't without complications. Marcos's past, marked by a messy divorce and questionable reputation, loomed over them. His divorce had been filled with bitter arguments and public confrontations. Gossip around his law firm painted him as reckless in his personal choices. His ex-wife had accused him of infidelity and prioritizing his career over their marriage. Their split had left Marcos with a reputation for being a playboy, someone who couldn't be trusted to commit.

In the professional arena, whispers of unethical practices dogged Marcos. Clients praised his sharp legal mind, but murmurs about how he achieved his victories persisted. Rumors of bending rules and exploiting legal loopholes followed him, casting shadows over his accomplishments. Despite his charm, these doubts about his character were a constant undercurrent in their relationship. Camila was drawn to his vibrancy, but she couldn't entirely ignore the red flags.

Camila tried to keep their affair hidden from everyone, especially Nic. But as the connection grew stronger, so did the risks they were taking. Late-night rendezvous and secret texts became harder to explain away, and Camila began to live in constant fear of being discovered.

The turning point came one afternoon when Marcos pressed Camila for more than just secret meetings. He wanted her to leave Nic and fully commit to him.

"I can't keep living like this," he told her, his voice thick with desperation. "We could be together, truly together."

But Camila hesitated. Despite everything, she couldn't bear to destroy her marriage entirely. Marcos confessed he didn't want to take care of another man's children, believing that since she was an absent mother, she would be okay with leaving Nic and her children. Camila was taken aback.

"No, Marcos. I can't abandon my kids. They need me, even if it doesn't seem that way. I can't just walk away from them," she said, her voice trembling.

Marcos's expression hardened. "If you stay, you'll be stuck in that life forever. We could have a fresh start, just us."

Camila shook her head, tears streaming down her face. "I can't do that to them. I can't do that to Nic. This affair has already caused enough damage."

"Where does that leave us, Camila? What has this relationship been about? A mere fling?"

Realizing the depth of her struggle, Marcos fell silent. The tension hung in the air, heavy with unspoken truths. Camila knew she had to make a choice, but the path forward was anything but clear.

That night, Camila sat alone in her bedroom, the weight of her decisions pressing heavily on her shoulders. After five months of their affair, the stress of living a double life was taking its toll. She felt torn between two worlds, unsure where to turn. She sent an urgent message to her faithful friend Rose: "I need to talk. It's serious. Can we meet for lunch tomorrow?"

Rose replied quickly, her curiosity piqued. "Sure, what time? What's so urgent?"

"Noon will work. I have to tell you in person. Not via text. See you tomorrow at our favorite spot."

The next day, Rose arrived at the restaurant, anxiety evident. "Hey Camila, what's up? You've had me on pins and needles all day."

Camila took a deep breath, her heart pounding. "Rose, I need to tell you something."

Rose leaned in, eyes wide. "Come on, spill it. What's going on?"

Camila glanced around nervously. "Remember that event at the law firm? The lawyer, Marcos, I met that night?"

Rose nodded. "Yeah, what about him?"

Camila's voice dropped to a whisper. "I've been seeing him. For the last five months."

Rose's eyes widened, her hand flying to her mouth. "Oh my God, Camila. Are you serious? Five months? You never mentioned a word about it. But now I understand why you haven't been as available."

Camila nodded, tears welling up. "It's been... intense. I'm sorry, Rose. I didn't want anyone to know about this affair. It's not something I'm proud of, but he makes me feel alive in a way I haven't felt in years. We go dancing, he's always eager to go out. Unlike Nic, who just wants to stay home."

Rose's expression softened, concern mixing with understanding. "But Camila, what about Nic? And the kids?"

Camila looked down, her voice trembling. "I know. I know it's wrong. But Marcos... he makes me feel like I can escape. He says we could be happy together, without worrying about the consequences."

Rose reached across the table, taking Camila's hand. "Camila, you have to think about your family. This isn't just about you and Marcos. Are you really willing to give all of that up?"

Camila's eyes filled with tears as she squeezed Rose's hand. "I don't know, Rose. I'm so confused."

Rose sighed, her voice gentle but firm. "Do you know what Marcos really wants? Is he looking for a future with you, or just enjoying the thrill?"

Camila bit her lip, her mind racing. "I don't know. He talks about a future, but..."

"But what? What demands is he placing on you?"

"Rose, Marcos talks about a future for us but without the children."

"Oh my God, Camila, this can't be. Is there any way you and Nic can work on your marriage?"

Rose nodded, giving Camila's hand a reassuring squeeze. "You need to think about what you want, Camila. What do you value more: the stability of your family or the passion with Marcos?"

Camila sat back, lost in thought. "I don't know. I need to figure this out."

As she stared out of the restaurant window, her mind raced as she thought about her current situation.

The affair with Marcos had created a deep rift, even affecting the children as she spent more time away from home. No longer the caring wife and mother she once was, Camila felt detached from her family, always irritable and bored when at home. Family evenings or activities with Nic and the children brought no joy. Distancing herself further, she felt liberated in another world, free from family responsibilities and daily worries. Nic's stability, love, and the children now felt like burdens, obstacles holding her back from the life she thought she wanted.

She was running out of excuses to leave the house, telling Nic she had errands or was meeting friends for lunch. It scared her how easily she lied, making up excuses and covering her tracks, fully aware this behavior could lead to the destruction of her family. Her entanglement with Marcos deepened. She knew it was dangerous and couldn't last forever, but she couldn't bring herself to end it. She wasn't ready to give up the way Marcos made her feel. It was probably only a matter of time before the truth came out, but until then, she was determined to live in the moment and hold on to the excitement Marcos brought into her life. Did she really want to go back to that boring existence?

Camila was so engrossed in thought that Rose had to wave her hands in front of her to get her attention. "Hello, anybody home? Earth to Camila."

Camila snapped back to the present. "I'm sorry, Rose."

Rose smiled softly. "You don't have to do it alone. I'm here for you, whatever you decide. I know this is difficult and you have some decisions to make. Just remember what's at stake here: your marriage, your family, those beautiful children who need a mom."

Camila took a deep breath, feeling the weight of her emotions. "Thank you, Rose. I really needed to talk about this. I have a lot to think about, and it helps knowing you're here for me."

Rose squeezed her hand, offering a reassuring smile. "Always, Camila. Take your time, and remember, you don't have to figure this out alone."

Camila nodded, feeling a flicker of hope. "I appreciate that more than you know. Let's catch up again soon."

They embraced before parting ways, each aware of the arduous journey Camila faced but bolstered by the strength of their friendship.

As Camila sat alone in her living room that evening, the weight of her decisions bore down on her. The thrill and excitement of her affair with Marcos were now overshadowed by the daunting realization of what she stood to lose. Her mind drifted back to Rose's words, "You have to think about your family." The guilt gnawed at her, a constant reminder of the betrayal she had committed.

She glanced around the room, her eyes lingering on the family photos that adorned the walls. Memories of happier times, moments filled with laughter and love, now felt like distant echoes of a life she had slowly let slip away. The choice before her seemed impossible: to continue living a lie with Marcos, chasing fleeting moments of passion, or to confront her demons and fight for the family she had nearly abandoned.

Her phone buzzed, snapping her out of her reverie. It was a message from Marcos, filled with promises of a future together. But as she stared at the screen, the words felt hollow. The children's laughter from upstairs pierced the silence, a poignant reminder of the stakes involved.

Taking a deep breath, she stood up, her resolve hardening. She had to make a choice that night—a choice that would define the rest of her life. The path ahead was uncertain, but one thing was clear: she couldn't continue straddling two worlds. She had to face the consequences of her actions and decide where her loyalties lay.

As the clock struck midnight, Camila headed upstairs, her heart heavy with the weight of her impending decision. She whispered a silent prayer for strength and guidance, knowing that whatever path she chose, there would be no turning back.

CHAPTER 7
SUSPICIOUS MIND

Nic, unaware of the affair but growing increasingly suspicious, noticed changes in Camila. She had become distant and secretive. He could feel her slipping away, but he didn't know why. His unease grew stronger. Something was clearly off.

The affair remained undetected for several months, but the strain of living a double life took its toll on Camila. She spent more time away from home, and when she was there, she was often distracted, lost in thoughts about Marcos. Nic noticed the changes in her behavior but didn't press her for answers, assuming she was just going through a phase.

Camila, once open and warm, had become distant and evasive. She was always on her phone, quickly locking it when Nic entered the room. Her late-night girls' nights and sudden errands multiplied, and her once predictable schedule seemed to change on a whim. Though Nic had never been the jealous type, he couldn't shake the feeling that something was terribly wrong.

At first, Nic tried to brush off his concerns. They had been married for close to a decade, and it wasn't uncommon for couples to hit rough patches. He acknowledged that Camila had become an absent mother and wife, but he trusted her. He knew that, unlike him, she needed external validation and exhilaration. In his heart of hearts, he didn't initially suspect an affair. Nic convinced himself that Camila was restless, perhaps because of his long work hours and the growing distance between them. He blamed himself for not being more present, for letting their relationship slip into routine.

While Camila and Marcos's affair continued, Nic began to notice the changes in his wife. She made constant excuses to avoid spending time with him. When she was home, she seemed preoccupied, lost in her thoughts. Nic tried to ignore it at first, convincing himself that Camila was simply busy or tired, but he knew something was wrong. The nights they used to spend talking and laughing were now filled with awkward silence. Their physical intimacy had faded as well, leaving Nic feeling rejected and confused. He began watching her more closely, trying to piece together the mystery. His suspicions grew, and soon he couldn't shake the feeling that there was another man in Camila's life.

One night, after Camila had gone to bed, Nic sat in the living room, his mind racing. Unable to shake the feeling that she was hiding something, he decided to check her phone while she slept. He knew it was wrong, that it would be a breach of trust, but his curiosity overpowered his better judgment. His heart pounded as he unlocked her phone and scrolled through her messages. At first, there was nothing out of the ordinary: conversations with friends, family, coworkers. But then he stumbled upon a string of messages from a contact named XOXO and a number he didn't recognize. The texts were vague but filled with affectionate undertones. They spoke of meeting in secret, stolen moments, and longing for each other. Nic felt a knot tighten in his stomach. His worst fears were coming true.

The next morning, Nic demanded to know who she had been texting. Ever the skilled manipulator, Camila acted shocked and hurt by his accusations. She denied everything, claiming the messages were innocent conversations with friends. She turned the tables on him, accusing him of being paranoid and controlling. "You could've just asked me, and I would have gladly shown you my phone and told you whatever you wanted to know."

Nic took a deep breath, trying to steady his emotions. He knew pressing further might escalate the situation. "Alright, Camila," he said, his voice calm but strained. "I'll take your word for it. But we need to work on our communication. This secrecy and distance between us can't continue if we want this marriage to work."

He turned and walked away, leaving Camila alone with her thoughts. Nic's mind raced with doubt and suspicion, but he knew that confronting her again without concrete evidence would only lead to more conflict. After he left, Camila deleted all messages with Marcos and his contact information from her phone.

The confrontation left Camila shaken. Her heart pounded as she denied his accusations, assuring him that everything was fine. But the look in his eyes told her he wasn't convinced. That night, as she lay beside him, a wave of guilt nearly broke her. She knew she was hurting the man who had loved her faithfully, who had given her a family and a life she had once cherished. Yet even with that realization, she couldn't shake the pull toward Marcos. The affair had become more than a mere fling; it was a consuming passion.

Nic stayed vigilant, hoping the truth would reveal itself in time. His suspicions grew with each passing day as he noticed Camila's frequent absences, sudden enthusiasm for the gym, and emotional detachment. Two weeks after the initial confrontation, his patience had worn thin. Nic had been watching her closely, and his suspicion reached a boiling point. When she arrived home late from work again, he was waiting for her at the kitchen table, ready to confront her.

"Where were you?" he asked, his voice tense with barely concealed anger.

Camila hesitated, her eyes darting around the room as she tried to come up with an excuse. But Nic wasn't interested in lies. "Don't lie to me, Camila. I know something's going on."

"I told you I was at the gym," she replied, trying to keep her voice casual.

"I know you weren't at the gym," Nic said, his voice rising. "You don't look like someone who's just worked out or showered. Plus, the gym closed hours ago. So, where have you been all evening?"

Camila considered confessing everything—the affair, her feelings of neglect, and how she had found solace in Marcos. But instinctively, she doubled down on her lies. "You're being paranoid," she shot back. "Just because I have a social life with friends and enjoy going out doesn't mean I'm doing anything wrong."

"Camila, this has nothing to do with having friends and fun. This is about the fact that you are neglecting your responsibilities to this household and your children. We have children who need us. You're acting like you're single with no responsibilities."

"Nic, you have no idea how suffocating it is to feel trapped. I need some space, some time to remember who I am outside of being a wife and a mother. I'm not trying to be single; I just need to breathe."

"Excuse me! Did you say suffocating? Trapped? Need space?" Nic mocked. "Enough with the excuses, Camila. This is about our responsibility for those two children who need parents and won't understand that you feel suffocated or trapped. Get your priorities straight. Your primary responsibility is being a mother."

Camila knew he was right and didn't respond, simply looking down in shame.

"You want to keep insisting that you were at the gym? That's fine, but don't think I'm stupid or naïve enough to believe you. Go ahead, don't tell me where you've been all evening and with whom. But let this serve as a warning: I am fed up with you and your immature behavior. It's time to grow up, Camila, or this marriage is not going to survive."

With that, Nic walked away, leaving her alone in the kitchen. Their argument had escalated, voices echoing through the house. Despite his suspicions, Nic had stopped short of directly accusing her of an affair. The fight ended in icy silence, with him retreating to his office and Camila to their bedroom.

After the confrontation, Camila retreated to her room, her heart pounding with fear and guilt. She felt trapped, her thoughts racing as she tried to figure out how to salvage the situation. The look of hurt and suspicion in Nic's eyes haunted her, and the weight of her deceit threatened to crush her. As she lay on the bed, tears streaming down her face, she realized that her lies were unraveling faster than she could manage.

The affair was taking its toll on Camila's life. She felt constantly torn between her duty to her family and her desire for Marcos. She became distant, her mind often wandering to thoughts of him even when she was at home with her children. She tried to hide the strain, but Nic sensed the change. His loving wife, once so attentive, seemed distracted.

Despite his suspicions, Nic wanted to trust Camila. His intuition grew stronger by the day, sensing something was wrong but unaware of her betrayal. Desperate for answers, he put a GPS tracker on her car to know where she went after work. She was rarely home and had no good explanation for her absences.

Checking her phone was a desperate act for answers. When he found the incriminating messages, his heart broke. The woman he loved, the mother of his children, was living a double life. The pain was almost unbearable. Even after confronting Camila, Nic struggled with his emotions. He wanted to believe her denials, to hold on to hope that their marriage could be salvaged. But the evidence was undeniable, and the trust between them was damaged.

The GPS tracker was a last resort to confirm his suspicions. Each new revelation felt like a dagger to his heart, confirming Camila's betrayal. Yet, amidst the anger and hurt, Nic also felt deep sadness for the life they had lost and the uncertain future.

Nic felt a profound sense of betrayal and confusion. He had always trusted Camila implicitly, believing in their bond. Discovering her deception shattered that trust, leaving him grappling with anger, sadness, and self-doubt. He questioned his actions, wondering if his long work hours and emotional distance had driven her away. The realization that he might have contributed to her unhappiness weighed heavily on him. Watching Camila become more distant and secretive, Nic felt helpless. He wanted to reach out, to bridge the gap, but didn't know how. His attempts to engage her were met with evasiveness or irritation, deepening his isolation.

The first few days of tracking provided little insight—Camila's car followed usual routes, with occasional stops at familiar places. Soon, however, the tracker revealed patterns Nic couldn't ignore. One evening, instead of heading home after work, Camila's car stopped at a bar on the other side of town, remaining there for hours. His heart sank as his worst fears were confirmed.

Over the next few weeks, the tracker painted a clearer picture. Camila's car frequently visited the same bar, a friend's house known for wild parties, a townhouse in Alexandria, Virginia, just outside Washington, D.C., and even a secluded spot by the river. Each location told a story of a life Nic was not part of—a life filled with the excitement and recklessness Camila craved.

Armed with this information, Nic felt a mix of anger, betrayal, and sadness. He knew he had to confront Camila but also understood this was a pivotal moment for their family. One evening, after putting the children to bed, he sat her down and showed her the GPS tracker data. Her initial reaction was defensive, but as Nic calmly laid out the facts, her defenses crumbled. She admitted to feeling trapped and unhappy, seeking solace in a lifestyle that ultimately left her emptier and more lost. The confrontation was painful but brought a moment of raw honesty that had been missing from their relationship for years. The revelations forced both Nic and Camila to face their reality.

"You know, Nic, your drinking is part of the reason I started going out so much. I needed an escape from this mess," Camila said angrily, turning to face him.

Nic sighed. "I know, Camila. My drinking didn't help. But we both made mistakes. We both need to change."

"Yes, Nic. I know we can make a difference in our relationship and rekindle what we once had. I'd really like to go back to the passion we once shared."

Nic looked at her, his resolve strengthening. "It's going to take time, but I'm willing to work on it if you are."

Camila nodded, a glimmer of hope in her eyes. "I'm willing. Let's do this together."

They embraced, both aware of the long road ahead but ready to take the first step toward healing. They decided to seek counseling, both individually and as a couple, to address their issues and find a way forward. Nic committed to getting sober, and Camila committed to being a better wife and mother. Nic's unwavering commitment to their family and Camila's willingness to confront her demons became the foundation for their healing journey.

While the path ahead was uncertain, the honesty and transparency from that difficult discussion gave them a chance to rebuild their relationship on firmer ground. For the sake of Adrián and Celina, they both knew they had to try.

Later that evening, as Camila sat alone in her bedroom, she had decided that she would give her marriage a chance and committed to letting Marcos know her decision.

As she contemplated her future, she received a message from Marcos: "I miss you. When can I see you again?"

Her heart raced as she typed her response, her fingers trembling. "I need to talk to you."

They met at their usual spot, a secluded corner of a nearby park. Marcos greeted her with a warm smile, but his eyes betrayed his anxiety. "What's going on, Camila?"

Taking a deep breath, she looked into his eyes. "Marcos, we need to talk about us... about the future."

Marcos's expression turned serious. "What do you mean?"

Camila hesitated, the words caught in her throat. She had intended to end things, to tell him she was choosing her family, but seeing him now, she couldn't bring herself to do it. "I... I don't know if I can keep doing this."

Marcos stepped closer, his voice soft yet insistent. "We can make it work, Camila. Just you and me. We don't need anything or anyone else."

Unable to keep the charade, Marcos confronted her, demanding a decision. He couldn't continue in the shadows and needed to know if she was willing to leave her marriage and start anew. The ultimatum left her reeling, torn between her loyalty to her family and her passion for Marcos. She was terrified of the consequences but also wanted the freedom he offered. Camila's mind was in turmoil, weighing risks and rewards of each choice. She thought of her children and how they would be affected. She loved them deeply and knew that leaving Nic would devastate them. Yet her heart ached for Marcos, who represented an uncertain but exciting future.

Torn between her love for her family and the passion she felt for Marcos, Camila made a decision she knew was temporary. "I need more time, Marcos. Please understand."

Marcos nodded, a mixture of relief and frustration. "Take all the time you need. Just remember, I'm here for you."

Despite her commitment to making her marriage work, when the time came to speak with Marcos, she couldn't go through with it. She decided to string Marcos along and continue the affair a little longer, unable to give up the excitement of their relationship. As they parted ways, Camila felt a pang of guilt but also a strange sense of comfort in knowing she hadn't closed the door on this part of her life just yet. She knew her choices would have consequences, but for now, she was caught between two worlds, unable to fully commit to either.

In the end, she couldn't bring herself to choose. She told Marcos she needed more time, pleading with him to understand the complexity of her situation. He agreed reluctantly, but Camila could see the frustration in his eyes. His patience was running thin, and her indecision was pushing him away. The tension between them had reached a breaking point, and she was caught in the middle, paralyzed by fear and desire.

Driving back home, Camila replayed her discussion with Marcos, which had not progressed as planned. Their connection had intensified to the point where casual meetings weren't enough. They had begun talking about their future, daring to imagine a life together. Marcos had even proposed that they leave everything behind. The idea was thrilling and terrifying, promising freedom at an unimaginable cost.

For a fleeting moment, Camila pictured a life free from her marriage, free to love openly. But the reality was daunting. How could she abandon her family, her children? The guilt and shame warred with the desire in her heart, and she felt trapped between two worlds. She weighed the options, realizing the enormity of what Marcos was asking. The conversation had ended with no clear answer, but the idea lingered. Camila knew that what they shared couldn't remain hidden forever. Sooner or later, they would have to confront the consequences.

As they parted that night, she had a sense of dread in her heart. She was no longer just flirting with danger; she was standing on the edge of a precipice, and one wrong step could send her entire life into chaos. She had to make a decision one way or the other.

Following their confrontation and renewed commitments the previous week, Nic wasted no time embarking on the road to sobriety. Determined to make a change, he poured out bottles of alcohol, attended support meetings, and spent more time with the children. Over the next year, he became more present, attempting to rebuild trust and reconnect with his family.

Meanwhile, Camila's actions remained contradictory. Though she had agreed to work on their marriage, she was often sneaking out at night, returning home late, and missing important family moments. Her feelings toward Nic grew more conflicted. She resented him for making her feel guilty and for not understanding her unhappiness. In her mind, Nic had driven her to the affair. If only he had been more attentive, more loving, more present, and agreed to move back to New York, none of this would have happened.

The household dynamics were tense and fragile. While Nic focused on mending their relationship, showing unwavering commitment to their family, Camila struggled with her own feelings and actions, caught between the life she had and the life she desired.

Adrián and Celina sensed the tension. Adrián, now old enough to perceive the strained atmosphere, became quieter, often retreating to his room. Celina, still too young to fully understand, clung to Nic more, seeking comfort from his newfound presence.

Nic's dedication to improving himself and his marriage was evident. He worked diligently on his sobriety, creating a stable environment for the children. He attended every school event, cooked meals, and made sure to spend quality time with Adrián and Celina. Nic's actions were his way of showing love and commitment, even when words failed him.

Nic was committed to mending his marriage, going out of his way to make things better and arranging romantic evenings. They even tried counseling, which Camila reluctantly agreed to, but during the first session, she was closed off and insincere, refusing to acknowledge problems in the marriage. Nic decided not to continue wasting his time. No matter what he did, his efforts seemed to make no impression on Camila. She remained cold and distant.

Camila, on the other hand, grappled with her sense of guilt and desire for freedom. She attended a few of the counseling sessions but remained emotionally distant. Her nights out with Marcos continued, leaving Nic in a state of constant worry and frustration.

The honesty and transparency that emerged from their confrontation provided a glimmer of hope, but it was clear the path to healing would be rocky.

One evening, as Nic tucked Adrián and Celina into bed, he lingered in the doorway, watching them sleep peacefully. The silence of the house contrasted starkly with the turmoil of their lives, but it held a promise of new beginnings. Camila stood in the hallway, her eyes meeting Nic's. They exchanged a tentative smile, both aware of the uncertain journey ahead but committed to taking it together.

As Nic turned off the lights, he whispered a silent vow to himself. No matter how long it took, he would fight for his family and the love they once shared. The path to redemption was fraught with challenges, but in the quiet moments of the night, there was a glimmer of hope that they could find their way back to each other.

CHAPTER 8
SHATTERED VOWS

The breakdown of their marriage was marked by intense arguments and emotional confrontations. Nic, his patience worn thin, finally confronted Camila about her behavior. The argument was explosive, shattering the fragile peace they had maintained for their children. Years of resentment and unspoken pain erupted, leaving their relationship hanging by a thread.

Nic, still unaware of Camila's affair with Marcos, remained devoted to his family, believing he was doing everything to keep them happy. He failed to see that Camila's satisfaction with family life was gradually fading, replaced by fascination with the life Marcos offered. The changes in her behavior—her growing distance, the late nights—were either ignored or attributed to life's stresses. As time passed with no improvement, Nic's hope began to fade. He realized there was nothing left to fight for. Exhausted, he seriously considered initiating divorce proceedings, seeing it as the only escape from his lonely, loveless life.

One year after their agreement, Nic sat on the couch, depleted. The dim living room light cast shadows across his face, highlighting the worry lines etched deeply into his features. He glanced at the clock, its ticking a constant reminder of the late hour. Camila stumbled in, clearly having been out partying.

"Camila, where have you been? It's 2 a.m. The kids were asking for you," Nic said, frustration evident in his voice.

"I needed a break and went out with friends," Camila replied defensively, avoiding his gaze.

"A break? You promised you'd stop this. You said you'd be a better mother," Nic said, his voice rising.

"I'm trying, Nic. It's not easy," Camila shrugged dismissively.

Nic ran a hand through his hair in exasperation. "I've kept my promise, Camila. I stopped drinking. I've been here for the kids. But you... you haven't changed at all."

His journey to sobriety had been long and arduous. He remembered the nights spent in a haze, the mornings filled with regret. The road to recovery was challenging, but he persevered, driven by love for his children and the desire to be a better man. Sobriety had cleared his perspective, giving him the strength to confront his marital issues, but it also made him realize he couldn't save Camila from herself.

"Don't you dare judge me! You think you're so perfect now?" Camila yelled, her face flushed.

"I'm not perfect, Camila. But I'm trying. And I can't keep doing this alone. The kids deserve better," Nic replied calmly, his voice steady despite his inner turmoil.

"I'm doing my best, Nic. I really am," Camila sobbed.

"Your best isn't good enough. Not for them. Not for us. I can't keep living like this. I think it's time we end this," Nic said softly, his voice breaking.

"What are you saying?"

"I'm saying I want a divorce. I've given you ten years, Camila. Ten years of trying to make this work. But I can't do it anymore."

"You can't just give up on us!" Camila cried. "Please give me another chance. I promise I'll change. Don't give up on me. Don't give up on us."

"I'm not giving up. I'm choosing to move forward. For the kids. For myself," Nic said sadly, his voice heavy with resignation.

"What about me? Nic, please help me keep our family together," Camila whispered, trembling. "I was wrong. Please let me make things right. We can be what we were before. Remember those college days, the dreams, the love? I know I've made promises before, but this time I won't let you down. I swear I'm serious. I know you still love me, and I love you. For the sake of our children, let's not throw away everything we've built."

Nic paused, his mind racing. He thought about the years of broken promises, the nights spent hoping for a change that never came. His heart ached at the thought of giving her another chance, fearing more disappointment. After a long silence, he looked at Camila, his resolve wavering. "Camila, this will be your last chance." His voice was barely above a whisper. "If you can't get it together, you'll need to find your own way. I hope you do, because I can't be the one to save you."

Camila stormed out to the porch, claiming she needed fresh air. The house shuddered as she slammed the door behind her, leaving silence in the wake of their explosive argument. Nic stood rooted in place, his heart pounding with a cocktail of anger, sadness, and bone-deep exhaustion

He found the children in Adrián's room. Celina had sought refuge with her brother, who held her close, both their faces pale with worry. Kneeling before them, Nic worked to keep his voice steady, masking his own turmoil.

"It's going to be okay," he whispered, gathering them into his arms. "I promise." He stayed until their breathing evened out in sleep, then carried Celina to her own room, each gentle step an effort to preserve their sense of safety.

Later, after calming down a bit on the porch and reflecting on her argument with Nic, Camila walked back into the house. She grabbed a bottle of water from the kitchen, her mind still racing with guilt and confusion. Then, she went straight to the bedroom. She knew the argument had been a breaking point, and the reality of her actions weighed heavily on her. As she sat on the edge of the bed, tears streaming down her face, she felt the full impact of the decisions she had made.

After tucking in the children, Nic retreated to the living room. He sank into the couch, staring at the wall as reality settled around him: their marriage was beyond repair. Any decision now would have to center on his children's well-being.

The night stretched on, with Nic and Camila processing their grief in separate corners of what had become a battlefield. The house that once rang with laughter now held only echoes of their shattered family. The path ahead remained unclear but change loomed inevitable.

Nic's patience and unwavering love for his family were more than just virtues; they were the quiet strength that held everything together. While Camila saw his patience as a weakness, it was actually his resilience shining through. This misinterpretation highlighted the tragic miscommunication that can unravel even the strongest of bonds, leading to profound consequences.

Whenever Camila compared Nic to Marcos, she couldn't help but feel turned off. Nic seemed weak in her eyes, lacking the killer instinct that Marcos possessed. This contrast only fueled her dissatisfaction. She yearned for the excitement and assertiveness that Marcos brought into her life, and in doing so, she overlooked the depth of Nic's love and dedication. This skewed perception deepened the rift between them, causing Camila to misinterpret Nic's true strength and see it as a flaw rather than the anchor it was for their family.

As the first light of dawn began to seep through the curtains, Nic and Camila both found themselves wide awake, lost in their thoughts. The house was silent, but the tension was palpable. Nic knew he had to be strong for his children, to provide them with the stability they needed. Camila, on the other hand, was torn between the life she had and the life she wanted.

Nic made a silent vow to fight for his family, to do whatever it took to create a safe and loving environment for Adrián and Celina. He knew it would be a long and difficult journey, but he was prepared to face it head-on.

Camila, too, felt the weight of her decisions. She knew she had to make a choice, and that choice would define the future of her family. As the day began, she resolved to confront her actions and take responsibility for the path she had chosen.

The road ahead was uncertain, filled with challenges and tough conversations, but one thing was clear: both Nic and Camila were determined to find a way forward, for the sake of their children and their own peace of mind.

CHAPTER 9
THE MOMENT OF RECKONING

Predictably, Camila maintained her best behavior for about a month. She came home straight after work, engaged with the children, and participated in family dinners and game nights. However, after that first month, Nic began to notice changes in Camila's behavior. Their intimacy grew distant, and she started slipping back into her old habits. She often avoided Nic's eyes and made mysterious phone calls she didn't want him to overhear.

Camila's actions stemmed from a belief that Nic's devotion to their family would never waver, no matter how far she pushed the boundaries. She believed that appeasing Nic for a month would keep him hooked. Camila, a beautiful woman, overestimated how far her beauty would take her. She saw herself as a twelve out of ten, while she considered Nic a six who would never have the guts to leave her or move on. This misconception gave her the perceived freedom to behave recklessly. The argument, intense as it was, didn't prompt serious change in her because it reinforced her belief that Nic would always be there, absorbing the impact of her actions.

In her mind, Nic's tolerance was a sign of weakness rather than resilience. She misinterpreted his unwavering patience and love as a lack of resolve, which emboldened her to keep testing the limits. The reality of her actions only became clear when Nic finally confronted her with the harsh truth and threatened divorce. This shook her out of her illusion that he would endure anything without breaking. His decision to seek counseling and set boundaries marked a significant shift, making Camila see a side of Nic she hadn't seen before and forcing her to recognize the potential for real consequences.

Recognizing these signs, Nic's suspicions resurfaced and grew. His intuition had been telling him that Camila might be having an affair, but he had no proof. Despite the turmoil they'd experienced over the last few years, their life had not yet reached the breaking point that would propel Nic to move on and say, "No más."

One afternoon, Camila claimed she received an urgent call from Rose, saying she needed to see her about a personal issue. Using this as an excuse to leave the house, she hurriedly told Nic she was meeting Rose for an early dinner and had to leave quickly. Nic was immediately suspicious of these last-minute plans. Taking advantage of the children visiting their grandparents, Nic decided to act on his suspicions. He feigned nonchalance and bade her goodbye. As soon as she pulled out of the driveway, he quickly jumped into his car and followed from a distance. As he tailed her car, he noted she took a route that led into D.C., heightening his unease since Rose lived in Fairfax. His heart pounded, feeling like he was inching closer to a painful truth.

After twenty minutes, Camila stopped in front of The Ritz-Carlton in Pentagon City, handed the valet her key, and quickly walked to the entrance. Nic remained in his car, watching from afar, a growing sense of unease gnawing at him. His heart stopped when he saw Camila greet a man he didn't recognize. Tall, well-dressed, and exuding confidence, the man's familiarity with Camila was undeniable. When he leaned in to kiss her, Nic felt a surge of anger and betrayal. His hands clenched into fists, and he had to remind himself to breathe. The sight of his wife with another man confirmed his worst fears, filling him with a mix of rage, sorrow, and a deep sense of loss.

Nic considered confronting Camila outside the hotel, but what would that accomplish? She would deny it, or worse, cry and pretend to be sorry. He had seen that performance before, how easily she could switch between playing the victim and taking control. No, he wouldn't give her the chance to manipulate him.

He parked near the hotel, remaining in his car, his heart pounding, palms sweaty, breathing slowly and controlled. His rage boiled beneath the surface. He didn't have a plan for this unexpected scenario, so he had to think quickly. Nic's hands gripped the steering wheel so tightly his knuckles turned white.

Unable to accept this betrayal, Nic decided to act. Once Camila and the man had disappeared into the lobby, he got out of the car and cautiously walked to the hotel, He watched them from a distance, his mind racing, struggling to comprehend the deceit. The image of Camila with this man was seared into his mind, and he felt a wave of nausea. His thoughts turned to his children, Adrián and Celina, and the impact this revelation would have on their lives.

Nic stood by the front entrance of the hotel, watching Camila from afar. He did not enter the lobby, which was empty, as he didn't want to be discovered. When he saw her and a man complete the check-in process and walk away from the front desk, he took a moment to formulate a plan. Determined to confront the situation and unveil the truth, he entered the lobby and approached the hotel's front desk where a young man was standing alone.

Taking advantage of the empty lobby, he said, "Hi there, my colleague just checked in, and I need to give him a message urgently. Can you please direct me to his room?"

"Are you referring to Mr. Marcos Medina, from the Martinez and Medina law firm?" the young man asked.

"Yes, that's correct," Nic replied.

"I can call his room and have him come down," the clerk offered.

"Oh no, please don't do that. Our company uses the same room for conferences, but I can't recall the room number. Can you please confirm which room he has checked in to? If he has to come down, it will cause a lot of issues, and I could lose my job. Please, I beg you to give me his room number, and I'll be in and out."

"I'm really not supposed to do that because of hotel regulations and privacy policies," the clerk hesitated.

Nic discreetly pushed a $100 bill toward the young man. "Okay, we won't tell anyone. No one has to know."

The young man looked around, then wrote the room number on a piece of paper, took the $100 bill, and handed the note to Nic. Nic thanked him and walked toward the elevator, heading to room 502.

As he walked, each step felt heavy, his heart pounding louder with every second. When he reached the fifth floor, he immediately located room 502. He stood by the door, hearing their laughter from inside—a sound that felt like a knife twisting in his heart. The betrayal was almost too much to bear.

Unable to contain his anger, he waited outside the room, his chest tightening, barely containing the rage that surged through him. His breath came in ragged bursts as he stood frozen just outside the hotel room door. His mind swirled in a chaotic storm of disbelief at Camila's betrayal. Every fiber of his being screamed at him to barge in and tear them apart. But something stronger, a primal instinct, held him back. He wasn't sure if it was shock or rage that rooted him in place, but it gave him a moment to think.

Despite the overwhelming emotions, Nic knew he had to stay composed. He thought of his children and the need to protect them from further pain. He recalled his experience during the days of alcohol withdrawal—the most difficult thing he had ever endured, and he did it for his children. Nic took a deep breath and tapped into that same source of strength that had carried him to sobriety.

Nic paced the corridor for a few minutes, each step heavy with tension. He took deep breaths, trying to calm his racing heart. With every second, his anger simmered, but he knew he had to stay composed. His mind raced, knowing Camila's manipulative ways too well. If she didn't see him confront her, she would weave a tale to turn the tables on him. He didn't want to give her the opportunity to dramatize her position as she usually did.

Determined to make his presence known, ensuring that Camila could not later deny the affair, Nic squared his shoulders and, with a heavy heart, knocked on the door, ready to confront the painful truth head-on.

A few seconds later, Nic heard a voice on the other side say, "Room service is here with that wine I promised." The door opened, revealing Marcos. At first, he wore a cocky grin, expecting to see room service. But upon seeing Nic, his expression faltered before he regained his composure. Nic saw Camila partially dressed in the background.

Marcos leaned casually against the doorframe, attempting to look at ease but betraying a flicker of surprise in his eyes. "You must be Marcos Medina. I'm Nic, Camila's husband," Nic said, speaking loud enough and positioning his body to make sure Camila saw him.

Nic felt a mixture of anger and sorrow but also a sense of resolve. This was the moment he had to confront, for the sake of his family and his own peace of mind. As Nic stood at the door, watching Camila's face transform from surprise to shock, a whirlwind of emotions surged within him. His heart pounded, each beat echoing the pain of betrayal.

He had hoped, against all odds, that his suspicions were unfounded, but now the truth was staring him in the face.

Camila's eyes widened, her face paling as she took a step back. Her trembling hands clutched at the fabric of her dress, as if it could shield her from the unfolding reality. She had been living a double life, and now it was all crashing down around her. The guilt and fear she had suppressed surged to the surface, threatening to overwhelm her.

Marcos quickly retreated into the room, giving Nic and Camila space to confront each other. He leaned against the wall, arms crossed, trying to maintain a facade of nonchalance, though his eyes betrayed a flicker of unease. Marcos was ready in case things turned violent, not wanting to be caught off guard nor let Nic hurt Camila. As long as they were just talking, he would remain uninvolved.

Nic's body language was tense, his fists clenched at his sides as he tried to control his emotions. He fought against the urge to lash out, knowing that violence would only make things worse. He knew Marcos didn't owe him loyalty, and if he got physical with Camila, Marcos would intervene, and the situation would quickly spiral out of control. Nic took a deep breath, his gaze never leaving Camila's.

"What are you doing here?" Camila asked, her voice trembling. She knew it was a weak question, but she needed time to develop an excuse. The look in Nic's eyes was one of profound hurt, cutting her to the core. She wanted to stay calm, unsure of what Nic would do. Camila's heart raced as she felt the walls closing in. She had never seen Nic like this before—his usually calm demeanor replaced by a cold, menacing presence. There was no turning back now. With Nic's piercing gaze locked on her, Camila felt the weight of her guilt crash down. She could no longer deny the truth, nor bear the thought of continuing the web of lies and deception that had ensnared her.

"I could ask you the same thing, Camila," Nic replied, his voice cold. "How long has this been going on?"

Camila swallowed hard, her eyes darting to Marcos, who stood silently watching the exchange with a smug expression. "Nic, please, let's talk about this somewhere else," she pleaded, her voice barely above a whisper.

"No, we're talking about this now," Nic insisted, stepping closer. "How long?"

When she didn't respond, he yelled and repeated his question with a firm and determined voice. "How long has this been going on?" he demanded, his voice steady but filled with hurt.

Camila's voice trembled as she replied, "About ten months." She couldn't meet his eyes, guilt weighing heavily on her. "I'm so sorry, Nic. I never meant for it to go this far."

Nic's resolve hardened. "Ten months," he repeated, shaking his head. "All those nights you said you were working late, at the gym, or out with friends. You were with him."

Camila nodded, tears streaming down her face. "I was unhappy, Nic. I felt trapped and suffocated. Every day felt like I was losing a piece of myself."

Nic's anger flared. "I was there, doing everything I could to hold our family together while you were out with him. Our kids need us both to be present and engaged. Did you ever stop to think what this will do to them? To me? To our family? Do you even care?" Nic shot back, his voice rising.

His words hit her like a punch to the gut. She realized she had jeopardized her children's stability and happiness. The weight of her actions pressed down on her, and she felt utterly lost.

The confirmation of her infidelity hung in the air like a storm cloud ready to burst. For a moment, Nic said nothing, his face unreadable, his emotions tightly controlled. Then, without warning, he kicked the door. Camila was startled by the bang, let out a shriek, and jumped back, afraid he was going to strike her. Marcos, standing on the sidelines, changed his nonchalant stance and took a step forward, ready to intervene if Nic made a move on Camila.

Nic then punched the door and spat, "How could you? After everything we've been through. After everything I've done for you. After I patiently supported you and your so-called depression. After I encouraged your career aspirations? Were you just playing me this entire time?"

Camila tried to say something as tears welled up in her eyes, but Nic wasn't finished and spoke over her. "You betrayed me," he continued, his voice rising with each word. "You betrayed our marriage, our children, our life together." Camila tried to apologize, but the words caught in her throat. There was nothing she could say to make it right.

Eight long months, at least that's what Camila had admitted to. Could it have been longer? Were there others? How many nights had Nic been out working late while Camila was tangled up with someone else? The thought made his blood boil.

Nic's gaze shifted to his wife. She looked so different from the woman he had married years ago, back when things were simpler, when they had made promises to build a life together. He thought he knew Camila, but he really did not know her at all. He had been judging her based on the woman he had married—trusting her and not believing she was capable of such deceit. Now, he saw that the woman he married had morphed into a deceitful, self-absorbed, and shameless person. The realization hit him like a punch to the gut.

Camila had checked out of their marriage long before tonight. Nic's stomach churned with disgust at the audacity of it all. He had sacrificed so much for their life, and she had thrown it away for a more exciting version of him. Nic gritted his teeth, forcing himself to breathe. He had his children to think about and needed to understand the full picture. Why hadn't Camila ended it if she was so dissatisfied?

His heart hammered in his chest. He was a patient man, but this level of betrayal was challenging his patience and ability to maintain control. Memories of her excuses—tired, stressed, not feeling it—flashed through his mind. She had found comfort elsewhere. Nic clenched his jaw.

A part of Nic wanted to lash out, to scream and demand answers. The anger was like a fire burning inside him, fueled by the image of Camila with another man. He felt deeply betrayed. Yet, amidst the anger, there was profound sadness. Memories of happier times flashed through his mind—their wedding day, the birth of their children, moments of laughter and love. He mourned the life they had built together, now shattered by her actions.

But overriding all these emotions was his concern for Adrián and Celina. He knew his actions would have lasting repercussions on their lives. He couldn't let his anger dictate his behavior. His children needed him to be strong and composed, to protect them from the fallout of this revelation.

Nic took a deep breath, trying to steady himself. This confrontation was especially painful and humiliating, particularly with Marcos standing there looking untouchable with his smug expression. But it was necessary and a turning point he had to traverse to move forward with his life. He had to put this painful situation behind him and forge a new path without Camila, not just for his own sake, but for his children. They deserved a stable, loving environment, free from the toxicity that had plagued his marriage.

He wasn't just angry; he felt a deep sense of humiliation. The thought of his neighbors, his friends, people who might have known what was happening behind his back only fueled his rage. He had been made a fool of. This was the moment he realized there was so much more to the story. Camila had been cheating. The suspicious texts he had glimpsed over the last few months, the secretive phone calls—he had dismissed them, brushing off his own insecurities. But now he understood this wasn't a one-time fling. Camila had been deceiving him for much longer than he had realized. He felt like such an idiot.

Looking into Camila's tear-filled eyes, he felt a mixture of pity and resolve. Their relationship was beyond repair, but he had to handle it with dignity and strength for Adrián and Celina. Nic walked away without a word, without looking back, leaving Camila at the door. He didn't care if she came home or not. He was done with her.

As Nic disappeared down the hallway, Camila stood frozen, her mind racing with guilt and panic. She watched him go, a sinking feeling of finality settling in. She knew she had crossed a line from which there was no return.

Camila had always felt a deep sense of dissatisfaction and restlessness in her marriage. The suburban life, the responsibilities, the feeling of being trapped—it all weighed heavily on her. Meeting Marcos had been like a breath of fresh air, an escape from the monotony and emotional void she felt at home. But now, seeing Nic's hurt and anger, she realized the full extent of her betrayal. She had to face the consequences of her decisions and actions.

Marcos, sensing her distress, stepped closer. "Camila are you okay?" he asked, his voice devoid of the earlier smugness.

Camila turned to face him, her eyes filled with regret. "No, I'm not okay. I've ruined everything," she whispered, her voice breaking.

Marcos reached out to touch her arm, but she pulled away. "I need to be alone," she said, her tone resolute. "I need to think about what I've done and where I go from here."

Marcos nodded, understanding that his presence was no longer comforting. "I'll be here if you need me," he offered, but Camila didn't respond. She was lost in her thoughts, grappling with the weight of her actions.

Camila, still grounded in the doorway, watched Marcos as he gathered his things. The reality of her situation hit her hard. She had to face the consequences of her betrayal and make some tough decisions about her future. The facade she had maintained for so long was crumbling, and there was no more hiding from the truth.

As Nic made his way back to his car, he felt a strange sense of relief mixed with sorrow. The confrontation had been brutal, but it was a necessary step towards moving on. He knew he had to focus on rebuilding his life for the sake of his children. They deserved better, and he was determined to provide them with the stability and love they needed.

The cool night air contrasted with his anger. This was the end of one chapter and the beginning of another. Determined to create a better life for his children, Nic felt a calm resolve. He sat in his car, waiting for his hands to stop shaking and his heart to calm.

Once he felt somewhat settled, Nic called his mother before heading home. He asked if she could keep the kids for a couple of days. He didn't want them to witness the emotional turmoil and commotion that would surely follow when Camila returned. Not ready to discuss the betrayal, he told his mother that he had to work, and Camila wasn't available. In reality, he needed time to recover from this devastating event and prepare for his separation from Camila. His mother, as usual, didn't question and simply said, "Sure, you know we love having the kids over."

As Nic drove home, he thought about the steps he needed to take to protect his kids and start anew. He would find a lawyer in the morning and begin untangling their lives. He couldn't change the past, but he was determined to build a better future. The road ahead would be long and arduous, but he knew he had to stay strong for Adrián and Celina. They deserved stability and love, free from the shadows of betrayal. With this resolve, he felt a glimmer of hope amidst the wreckage of his marriage.

CHAPTER 10
THE WEIGHT
OF BETRAYAL

Nic sank onto the living room couch, emotionally drained after the confrontation. The weight of Camila's betrayal hung heavy, suffocating him. He stared blankly at the wall, each memory of the day's events a fresh wound.

The house was eerily quiet as he alternated between pacing and sitting, his mind racing. The front door opened and closed softly. Camila entered, face pale and eyes reddened from crying. She hesitated before stepping into the room where Nic waited.

"Nic," she began, voice trembling. "I can explain."

He didn't shout, but his words dripped with pain and disappointment as he stood and started pacing, anger barely contained. "Explain? What is there to explain, Camila? I saw you with him. I followed you to that hotel. Do you have any idea how that felt? To see my wife, the mother of my children, with another man—in a compromising position?"

Tears streamed down Camila's face as she inched closer. "Nic, believe me when I say I love you and the kids more than anything."

"Camila, please don't call your hypocrisy love. You don't love anyone but yourself."

"Nic, I'm so sorry. I made a terrible mistake. Please, just let me explain."

Nic's fists clenched, knuckles whitening. Surging anger threatened to consume him, but he fought to maintain control. Taking a steadying breath, he refused to let his emotions spiral. "A mistake? You destroyed our family, Camila. You shattered the bond we had, broke every vow we made, and destroyed everything we built together."

Camila's mumbled justification was barely coherent. "It...it was a mistake. Marcos was just there when I felt trapped and suffocated. I didn't want to ruin our home life, honestly."

Nic's eyes flashed. "Again, you claim to have felt suffocated—as if that excuses your selfishness. Camila, your needs and desires blinded you to the damage you were causing. All you thought about was yourself."

His voice rose, and he could no longer hold back tears. Camila continued apologizing, but Nic no longer saw the person he once trusted.

Realizing the futility of denying the truth, Camila admitted her feelings for Marcos had grown beyond her control. "Nic, I...I'm guilty. You're right. I made a terrible mistake," she began, but Nic, overcome with anger and disbelief, cut her off.

"A mistake? You keep calling this affair—a mistake. Camila, an affair is a deliberate choice, not a mistake. You can't gloss over your wrongdoing by labeling it a mistake and expecting an apology to fix everything. I don't want to hear your excuses for why our world has imploded. Your declarations of accountability, regret, remorse—they mean nothing. You destroyed everything we built, everything we were. You betrayed me, betrayed our children. How can you call that a mistake?"

Camila knew justifications would fall on deaf ears. She lowered her head, unable to meet his gaze. "I can't justify myself, Nic. You deserve better," she whispered.

The intensity of his stare made her recoil, afraid he might lash out. "I can't justify my behavior. All I can do now is ask for a chance to show I've learned from my mistakes."

Nic stood in stunned silence, fists clenched. He took a steadying breath before speaking, each word laced with pain. "Camila, think about what you're asking. Why should I give you that chance? What do you expect—for me to forget everything that happened? Erase the nights I waited up for you, while you were with another man? Forget that I caught you in a hotel room with him?"

Tears streamed down Camila's face. "No, I don't expect that. I hope you can forgive me, not for what I did, but for the wife and mother I can be now that I've learned from my mistakes."

Nic shook his head, his expression a mix of disbelief and resignation. "Camila, you have a lot of nerve asking for another chance. I've heard your promises before. Every time you said you would change, every time you said things would get better. But nothing ever changes with you. It's always about you and how you feel, ignoring this family's needs. I'm done listening to hollow excuses and promises."

Nic thought to himself, "My mother was right. A leopard never changes its spots. What made me think she would change her behavior?"

Camila's sobs turned into wails as she realized the finality of his words. "No, Nic, please. Don't do this. I can change. I can—" Camila fell to her knees, her hands clasped together in desperation. "Please, Nic. Don't do this. Don't throw away everything we've built together in the last ten years. Think about the kids. They need both of us."

Nic's voice softened, but his resolve remained firm. "The kids need us both, but they also need stability and honesty. They need a home where they can feel safe and loved, not one filled with lies and betrayal."

Camila's tears continued to stream down her face as she tried to speak. "Nic, please believe me when I say that I regret the affair. I was thinking on the way home and realized that this experience has changed me. I am no longer the person I was yesterday. I don't want to live without you and the kids. I'm begging you for your forgiveness and love."

Nic's eyes flashed with anger, his voice steady but filled with hurt. "In hindsight, I now recognize that you've always treated me like I'm weak, like I don't have the guts to live without you. You believed I would forgive you for anything, that I'm trapped in your web." Nic took a step closer, his gaze intense. "But you were wrong. This experience has changed me in ways I never imagined. It shattered my trust and made me question everything I believed. No matter how much you cry, no matter how much you beg, I won't change my mind. I'm done with you."

Camila looked up at him, her eyes filled with despair. "What are you saying, Nic? Are you leaving me?"

Nic inhaled deeply, his heart heavy with the weight of his decision. "I'm saying that this marriage is beyond repair. Camila, I can't trust you anymore, and without trust, there's nothing left. I'm going to file for divorce and seek full custody of the kids. They deserve better than this."

Camila's sobs turned into desperate cries as she realized the finality of his words. "No, Nic, please. Don't do this. I can change. I can be better. Please forgive me."

Nic exhaled slowly, trying to calm his anger. "Camila, you can't ask for forgiveness—you have to earn it." He turned away, unable to bear the sight of her anguish. "It's too late, Camila. I've given you so many chances, and you've squandered every opportunity to save our marriage and family. I need to think about what's best for the kids and for myself. Divorce and each of us going our separate ways is the only viable option."

Completely exhausted and drained by the revelation of Camila's betrayal, Nic stood tall, his back straight and his chin up. He wasn't happy about what had transpired, but he was confident he had made the right decision. He had shed many tears, but his eyes were now dry, and he vowed this would be the last time he wept over this betrayal. Now that the truth was out, he had to move forward without Camila. He wanted nothing more to do with her and could no longer stay in this marriage.

Nic stopped pacing and sat across from Camila, his expression a mix of exhaustion and resignation. "Camila, I've done all I can. I gave it my best, but I guess my best wasn't good enough for you."

Camila looked at him, her eyes brimming with tears. "Nic, please don't say that."

"We always end up right back where we started," Nic continued, ignoring her plea. "It seems like nothing ever changes with you. I look at you now, and you seem like a stranger. How many times have we been here, wondering if we should stay together or get divorced?"

"The magic we had during our college years faded long ago," he said, his voice heavy with sadness. "I've tried to find a way to keep this family together, to make it right, but the harder I try, the further you pull away."

Camila's tears began to fall. "I know I've made mistakes, but I still love you."

Nic shook his head. "I've given everything, but it's like we're running in circles. We just keep messing it up. I'm done trying. This marriage doesn't have a chance."

Camila reached out to him, her voice trembling. "We can fix this, Nic. We can try again. We don't have to make a final decision now; we can go to therapy and give it time."

"Camila, you made your choice the moment you had an affair. Now, I'm making mine."

Camila's sobs grew louder, but Nic's resolve was unshakable. "It's over, Camila," he said quietly. "We need to let go for our own sake and for the sake of our children."

Nic turned to Camila, still kneeling on the floor, and said, "I've moved your belongings to the guest room. I don't want to see you or interact with you unless it's absolutely necessary and concerns the children. We can both stay in the house until you find a new place."

Camila stood abruptly, feeling abandoned. "You moved my things? When? And you decided to cast me out of my home? This house is as much mine as it is yours."

"As I was driving back from the hotel, I realized I can no longer live this way. This wasn't abrupt; it's the culmination of your actions over the last few years. As soon as I got back, I moved your things. I couldn't bear the sight of anything that reminded me of you and your affair. I also decided it would be best if you moved out."

Camila's eyes widened in shock. She was speechless.

"You're correct, this is also your house, but it is no longer your home. I will ensure you receive your share of the equity so you can rent or purchase a place of your own. In the last couple of years, you've acted like a guest, taking no responsibility. You've proven repeatedly that a home, family life, caring for the children, and maintaining a household is not what you want. Now you can go off and live the life you want with no strings attached."

Nic walked out of the room, leaving Camila to grapple with the consequences of her actions. She dropped to her knees in despair, her cries echoing through the house—a painful reminder of their shared past and the future now lost.

Once out of sight, Nic paused in the hallway, leaning against the wall as the weight of his decision settled in. He closed his eyes, taking a deep breath, convinced this was for the best. He wouldn't let Camila's outburst manipulate his emotions any longer.

He wanted to scream, to demand why she had thrown away everything they had built together. Instead, he retreated into silence; the words choking in his throat. Nic wondered if he had failed her somehow if there was something he could have done to prevent this. The questions haunted him, but the answers remained elusive. All he knew was that their life together had been irrevocably changed, and he was left to pick up the pieces of a shattered dream.

Nic realized their relationship had transformed irreversibly. He could no longer trust her or see her the same way. Gone were the days and nights spent together, their conversations, laughter, and dreams of the future. All these moments now seemed distant and unreal, part of a life that would never return. Everything that had once felt solid to him had collapsed in one evening.

As he stepped away from the living room, the cool night air from an open window hit his face, a stark contrast to the heat of his anger. A strange calm washed over him. This marked the beginning of a new chapter in his life. He knew the road ahead would be difficult, but he was determined to build a better life for his children. With each step, the weight of his decision transformed into a newfound resolve to move forward, stronger and wiser.

Nic walked into the kitchen, grabbed a bottle of water, and stared into space, knowing his life had changed forever. He hadn't just lost his family; he had lost a part of himself. The experience left him jaded and suspicious of everyone around him. Yet, in that moment, he felt a strange relief—everything was out in the open; there were no more secrets, no more lies.

Sitting in the kitchen, Nic was immersed in the painful realization that his worst fears had been confirmed. Their home, their life, their shared history—everything they had built together over the years—had fallen apart. Every detail of their relationship now reminded him of the betrayal. His wife hadn't just cheated on him physically; she had betrayed him emotionally, choosing another person for her thoughts, feelings, and secrets. The memories of their college days, once inseparable, now felt like a cruel joke.

As he walked up to his bedroom, the events of the day replayed in his mind. Nic thought about how many times he had suspected her of infidelity but had brushed these thoughts aside, not wanting to believe it. He remembered noticing her drifting away—the frequent absences, the nervousness, the new habits. Now, he saw not just the woman he had lived with but a person capable of lies, betrayal, and manipulation.

He couldn't shake the image of Camila with Marcos, the way she had looked at him with a spark long gone in their marriage. It gnawed at him, a constant ache that no amount of time seemed to dull. Nic stared at the empty side of the bed, the sheets cold and untouched.

He recalled when that space had been filled with warmth and laughter. Disgusted by Camila's betrayal, he changed the sheets before getting into bed.

Nic knew the road ahead would be difficult, but he was ready to take it. This day became the starting point of a new stage in his life—a life without lies and betrayal but with deep scars that would remain forever. After exposing Camila's actions, his life had changed dramatically.

CHAPTER 11
ECHOES OF REGRET

Camila sat on the edge of the bed in the guest room, her eyes red and swollen from crying. The room felt cold and unfamiliar, a stark contrast to the warmth of the bedroom she once shared with Nic. She clutched a photo of their family, her fingers tracing the smiling faces of their children. Lowering her head, Camila faced the reality of her exposed secret. Shame and guilt washed over her, yet she couldn't ignore the passion that had bound her to Marcos.

What started as innocent flirtation had become something deeper and destructive. Nic had been consumed by his career, leaving Camila feeling invisible and unappreciated. Marcos had noticed her, complimented her, and shared her interests in a way Nic hadn't in years.

Camila was torn by conflicting feelings—she felt guilty for destroying her marriage and betraying Nic's trust, yet memories of her heart fluttering with every meeting with Marcos haunted her. She relished his attention and admiration, something she hadn't felt with Nic for a long time. This internal conflict tore her apart.

Feeling exposed, Camila knew everything had changed. The secret passion that once excited her was now a source of pain. She knew their marriage had been in trouble, but she never imagined it would lead to this. She had to take full responsibility for the consequences of her actions.

How did I let it come to this? she thought, her heart heavy with regret. The memories of her affair with Marcos played in her mind like a haunting reel, each moment a reminder of her betrayal. She had been drawn to the excitement and the feeling of being desired, but now all she felt was shame.

Nic had once been the love of her life. Now, they were both trapped in the wreckage of her choices. Camila found herself staring at the ceiling, the silence echoing her regrets. She remembered the thrill of Marcos's charm, the escape from the monotony of her marriage. But that thrill had turned into a painful reminder of what she had lost.

She saw it in Nic's eyes every time he looked at her—an unspoken question, a silent accusation. The weight of her decisions pressed down on her, a constant reminder of the life she had shattered. She wondered if things could have been different if she had turned away from Marcos that first night or tried to mend her marriage. But those were dreams of a past that could never be rewritten. The damage was done, and all that remained was the cold reality of their fractured lives.

Her thoughts were interrupted by Nic's footsteps outside the door. She wanted to run to him, to beg for his forgiveness, but she knew it wouldn't be enough. She had heard the finality in his voice, seen the resolve in his eyes. He was done with her, and she couldn't blame him.

I've destroyed everything, she thought, tears streaming down her face. I've hurt the people I love the most. The thought of their children, caught in the crossfire of her mistakes, made her heart ache even more. She feared for their future, their stability now hanging by a thread. In a moment of desperation, she fell to her knees, hands clasped as she pleaded. "Nic, don't let this be the end of our marriage," she whispered to the empty room. "Let's keep the family intact so the children don't have to grow up in a broken home."

But deep down, she knew words alone wouldn't change anything. She had to show him, show everyone, that she could be better. That she could change. It was a long road ahead, and she wasn't sure if she could make it, but she had to try. For her children, for herself, and maybe, just maybe, for a chance to earn Nic's forgiveness.

When Rose had asked if she was willing to give up her family, Camila was undecided, captivated by her relationship with Marcos. But now that Nic had made the decision for her, she felt a deep sense of loss and helplessness. Perhaps it wasn't the outcome itself, but the fact that the choice was no longer hers to make. Her fate had been sealed, and she was no longer in control.

With the loss of control, Camila realized she had to face the consequences of her actions and choices. Her life had changed irrevocably, and she now had to navigate the path ahead, seeking a slim hope of redemption on the horizon.

On the other side of town, Marcos dealt with the aftermath of his actions. The confrontation replayed in his mind. He was still shaking, recalling the look on Nic's face, unsure of what Nic would do. Fortunately, Nic was not a violent man, and the confrontation did not end in disaster.

Marcos sat alone in his dimly lit apartment, the silence pressing down on him. He couldn't shake the image of Camila's hurt expression, the pain in her eyes cutting deeper than any words could. He glanced at his phone, hoping for a message or call from her. But the screen remained dark. What did I expect? he thought, running a hand through his hair. That she would leave everything behind and come to me?

He remembered the first time they had crossed the line from friendship to something more. It had felt exhilarating, like a forbidden thrill. The scent of her perfume, her laughter, the stolen glances—they were intoxicating. But now, the excitement had faded, replaced by Camila's guilt and regret. I never wanted to hurt anyone, he told himself, but the reality was unavoidable. He had played a part in destroying a family. He quickly dismissed that thought, not wanting to dwell on something he couldn't fix.

Marcos picked up a photo from the table. It was of him and Camila, taken during one of their secret getaways. They looked happy, carefree. But now, that happiness felt like a distant memory, overshadowed by pain and chaos. I should have known better, he thought. I should have stopped it before it went too far.

He wondered what Camila was doing now. Was she safe? Probably so—Nic did not appear to be a violent person. Marcos wasn't sure he would have been able to control himself in Nic's shoes. Was she with Nic, trying to mend their shattered marriage? Or was she alone, grappling with regret and sorrow? Marcos stood up and walked to the window, gazing out at the city lights. He felt a pang of loneliness, a stark contrast to the warmth and connection he had felt with Camila.

Maybe it's time to let go, he thought. Maybe it's time to face the consequences and move on. He didn't want to be part of a complicated love triangle; they rarely end well. Love triangles often lead to feelings of jealousy, mistrust, and betrayal, causing pain for everyone involved. They create a web of emotional entanglements that are difficult to navigate and often end in heartbreak and sometimes worse, as they can end in violence. Marcos leaned against the window frame, his arms crossed tightly over his chest. He sighed deeply, his shoulders sagging under the weight of his thoughts.

He had to admit he didn't want to deal with another man's children. He loved spending time with Camila but wasn't ready to become a stepdad. The responsibilities of a stepfather felt overwhelming. He enjoyed his freedom and wasn't ready to give that up. He was going to miss Camila. She was a lot of fun, and he had grown fond of her over the last ten months, even thinking they could have a future together. He ran a hand through his hair, feeling the tug of conflicting emotions. He had to give that some serious thought.

Marcos wanted to give Camila time to see where her marriage went. However, he doubted Nic would forgive her. He also wasn't sure if he wanted a life with a woman who had cheated on her husband. "After all, she might do the same to me," he thought, seeing Camila in a different light.

In the aftermath of the confrontation at the hotel, Marcos had changed. What was once filled with passion lost its luster as he became distant, preoccupied with his own problems. Alone in his apartment, he felt the weight of his actions. The excitement and passion had faded, leaving only the harsh reality of the choices he had made. He couldn't escape the image of Camila's hurt expression and the consequences that had unfolded.

Marcos sat on his couch, staring at the city lights. The thrill of the affair, the excitement of the forbidden—all had turned to ashes. He thought about the nights they had spent together, the mix of desire and affection in her eyes. Those memories were now tainted, overshadowed by the reality of their actions.

What now? he wondered. Was he really ready to take on the complications that came with Camila's life? He enjoyed his freedom and wasn't ready to become a stepdad. The responsibilities felt overwhelming. He remembered the nights they had spent together, the mix of desire and affection in her eyes. But those memories were now tainted by their actions.

He realized that he had been viewing Camila through rose-colored glasses. The affair had blinded him to the complexities and consequences. Once a cheater, always a cheater, he thought, seeing Camila in a different light.

It was time to move on, he concluded, with a clearer sense of re-solve. Having made up his mind to end the affair, Marcos contacted Camila and arranged to meet. During dinner at a place they had frequented, he approached her with a serious tone. "We need to talk," he said. Camila's heart sank, knowing what was coming. "I think we should end this," Marcos said bluntly. "It's not working anymore."

Camila felt a pang of sadness but wasn't surprised. The affair had caused more pain than pleasure, and deep down, she knew it was time to let go. "I understand," she replied, her voice barely above a whisper. With that, their relationship ended as abruptly as it had begun.

Marcos found a different path. While he grappled with the consequences of the affair, he began to focus on rebuilding his own life. The connection that once brought excitement and passion had become a burden, reminding him of a period he'd rather forget. Determined to move forward, Marcos embraced the freedom and simplicity of a life unencumbered by the complications of his past relationship with Camila.

However, the repercussions of the affair extended into his professional life. Marcos had to face the other partners at his firm, who were displeased with the scandal and its potential impact on their reputation. Management from Camila's firm had also reached out, expressing their disappointment and the strain this affair had placed on their business relationship. The once-amiable professional relationships he had enjoyed were now fraught with tension and distrust.

Camila, on the other hand, found herself isolated, her once vibrant connection with Marcos now a source of profound sorrow. She returned home, her heart aching with a sense of abandonment. In the silence of her room, she let her emotions flood through her. The tears came in waves, each one a reminder of the solace she thought she had found in Marcos, now gone.

She had believed that Marcos would be her escape, her comfort. But now, even that illusion was shattered. The weight of her actions pressed down on her, and the reality of her situation became unbearable. Her solace was supposed to be in Marcos, but now she was truly alone, grappling with the consequences of her betrayal.

As she faced her dark night of the soul, she realized the true cost of her actions. Her life was forever changed, marked by the scars of betrayal and the painful journey toward redemption.

Camila had destroyed everything she once held dear. The nights were the hardest, alone with her thoughts and the weight of her choices. Lying in bed, she realized, "I was searching for something I never lost. Everything that mattered in life was already mine, and I threw it away." She stared at the ceiling, the silence amplifying her regret. Camila was left with nothing—no marriage, no lover, no happiness.

Camila withdrew from the world, ashamed of what her life had become. The affair with Marcos had become common knowledge, turning her workplace into a hostile environment. Colleagues who once admired her now looked at her with disdain, their judgment making her job unbearable. She had embarrassed the firm with her scandalous behavior. Her boss had removed her from managing the Martinez and Medina account as the affair had reached management's ear. She was no longer trusted to represent the company with integrity.

Her neighbors eyed her like she was wearing a scarlet letter. Every corner of her life became tainted with pain and shame. The whispers, the icy stares, and the haunting memories of her time with Marcos were inescapable. Each day was a reminder of the life she had shattered.

To make matters worse, Camila found herself excluded from social gatherings and community events. Invitations that once filled her mailbox were now non-existent. Friends she thought she could rely on avoided her, their silence speaking louder than words. She felt like an outcast in her own neighborhood, the stigma of her actions clinging to her like a second skin.

At home, the reality of her choices weighed heavily on her. Her children, sensing the tension, grew distant, their innocent eyes filled with confusion and hurt. The family dinners that once buzzed with laughter were now silent affairs, the air thick with unspoken words. She longed to rebuild the trust she had broken, but the road to redemption seemed impossibly long and steep.

Camila knew she had to face the consequences of her actions and work towards rebuilding her life from the ground up. Each day was a struggle, but she vowed to find a way to make amends, even if it took a lifetime.

Nic's actions at the hotel marked a turning point in his life. Had he acted on his rage, the consequences could have been catastrophic—an explosive confrontation that might have ended in violence or legal repercussions, affecting the children. Instead, Nic chose composure, his controlled yet firm response to Camila's betrayal showing true strength.

In the days that followed, Nic grappled with the reality of his new life. The house felt emptier, the silence more pronounced. He couldn't escape the image of Camila with Marcos, but he knew he had made the right choice for himself and his children. The betrayal had shattered his trust, but it also revealed his resilience.

Every step forward felt heavy, but Nic was determined to rebuild. He focused on his children, providing them with stability and love. The nights were the hardest, memories of his marriage swirling in his mind. Yet, amidst the pain, he found a strange sense of clarity and purpose. He knew he had to be strong, not just for himself, but for Adrián and Celina.

The experience had changed him in ways he never imagined, shattering his trust and making him question everything he believed. Yet, it also made him realize the importance of integrity and dignity. Nic's ability to maintain his composure and make hard decisions became a beacon of strength for his children, showing them that even in the face of betrayal, one can choose a path of honor and resilience.

Nic's journey was far from over, but he faced it with a newfound resolve. He wasn't just reacting to the adversity; he was actively shaping his future, determined to create a life free from lies and filled with honesty and love.

As the echoes of the confrontation slowly faded, each character faced the harsh reality of their choices, forever altered by the events that transpired.

For Nic, the ordeal underscored the importance of integrity and resilience. His ability to confront betrayal with composure and dignity demonstrated that even in the face of profound pain, one can choose honor and strength. His journey to rebuild his life with honesty and love became a testament to the power of perseverance.

Marcos lamented the blowback he received from his partners as a result of the affair. The thrill had blinded him to the complexities and responsibilities that came with it, both personally and professionally. He underestimated the challenges of being involved with a married woman with children. Professionally, he faced the displeasure of his firm's partners, who were concerned about the scandal's impact on their reputation and the strain on their business relationship. These professional consequences weighed heavily on him, highlighting the necessity of accepting the repercussions of his actions and finding the courage to change.

Camila's journey was marked by isolation and regret. The weight of her choices left her grappling with the fallout, both personally and professionally. Her realization that she had thrown away everything that truly mattered served as a poignant reminder of the far-reaching impact of betrayal. The path to redemption was steep, but it began with acknowledging her mistakes and the desire to make amends.

Ultimately, this chapter serves as a powerful reminder that our actions have consequences, and the choices we make define our paths. Integrity, accountability, and the willingness to confront our mistakes are essential in navigating the complexities of life. The confrontation at the hotel was not just an end, but a beginning—a catalyst for each character to embark on a journey of self-discovery, growth, and finally, redemption.

CHAPTER 12
TRANSITIONING TO CO-PARENTING

After discovering Camila's betrayal, Nic accepted that their relationship was irreparably damaged. Determined to shield his children from further turmoil and provide stability, he began planning for a life without her. With a heavy heart, Nic meticulously outlined their new future, starting with separating their financial accounts, housing, and cell phones—everything they once held jointly. He reviewed his finances to ensure he could support Adrián and Celina on his salary alone. Consulting a financial advisor, he created a comprehensive plan, including budgeting, investments, and securing their future education. Establishing clear financial boundaries, he set up separate accounts and assets.

To ensure a gradual transition, Nic agreed to keep the family home and let Camila stay until she was financially stable enough to find her own place. This arrangement provided continuity for the children, allowing them to stay in their home, attend the same school, and maintain their friendships. However, living under the same roof presented emotional challenges, especially since Camila's betrayal made it difficult for Nic to even look at her.

Nic's thoughts became clearer and more independent. He stopped seeking Camila's opinion on anything. Despite his resolve, there were moments when Nic second-guessed himself. Late at night, memories of happier times with Camila flooded his mind. The thought of his children growing up in a broken home gnawed at him. He questioned whether he was making the right decision. These doubts added another layer of emotional complexity.

Sharing the house meant constant reminders of their broken relationship. Every interaction was fraught with tension, with Nic struggling with anger and hurt while Camila faced guilt and regret. Nic often retreated to his office or took long walks to avoid confrontation, while Camila spent most of her time in the guest room, trying to stay out of his way.

Custody was one of the most challenging aspects. Nic was determined that Adrián and Celina would stay with him. He knew Camila had been absent from their lives, and he understood their needs and routines. He refused to discuss shared custody, believing it was in the children's best interest to remain in a stable environment. Nic sought legal counsel to navigate the complexities of divorce and custody. He wanted to ensure his rights, and the well-being of his children were protected. The lawyer advised him on the steps to file for divorce and secure full custody. Nic gathered evidence of Camila's infidelity and neglectful behavior as a mother.

While focusing on the practical aspects, Nic couldn't ignore the emotional toll. The betrayal left deep scars, and he struggled with feelings of anger, sadness, and loss. He sought support from friends and family, who provided a listening ear and encouragement. Nic began to rebuild his life with a renewed sense of purpose, focusing on creating a stable environment for Adrián and Celina.

Maintaining normalcy for the children was challenging. Adrián and Celina sensed the tension and were confused, still oblivious to the reasons behind their mother staying in the guest room. They asked innocent questions that neither parent could answer without revealing the painful truth. This added another layer of complexity, as Nic and Camila had to navigate their own emotions while ensuring Adrián and Celina felt secure and loved.

Dinners were difficult. The once lively family meals were now quiet and tense, with forced smiles and stilted conversations. Nic found it hard to look at Camila without remembering her betrayal, and Camila felt the weight of her guilt with every glance Nic threw her way. The atmosphere was thick with unspoken words and unresolved emotions.

When Nic played board games with the children, they would ask if they should get mommy from the guest room so she could join them. Nic would reluctantly agree, telling them to go ask her, but he did not want her at the table. He did not want to see or interact with her.

Nighttime was the hardest. Nic would lie awake, the silence of the house amplifying his thoughts. He could hear Camila moving around in the guest room, a painful reminder of their fractured relationship. The house, once filled with warmth and laughter, now felt cold and empty. Each day was a struggle to maintain normalcy for the children, while Nic and Camila silently navigated their shattered world.

However, Nic began to see glimpses of hope and new possibilities. He started to envision a future where he and his children could thrive without constant turmoil. He took small steps towards rebuilding his life, finding solace in routines and moments of joy with Adrián and Celina. One evening, as he played a board game with the kids, their laughter filled the room, momentarily lifting the heavy cloud that had settled over their home. These moments provided Nic with the strength to keep moving forward.

Their journey toward co-parenting and rebuilding their lives was only beginning. The road ahead was uncertain and filled with emotional hurdles, but within the struggles lay the potential for growth, forgiveness, and perhaps, one day, understanding.

CHAPTER 13

TOO LITTLE, TOO LATE

Despite all the changes, Camila felt uneasy but remained hopeful that Nic would never follow through with the divorce. She believed he was bluffing, lacking the resolve to go through with it. His past forgiveness of her transgressions led her to think this time would be no different. Her delusional overestimation of her self-worth blinded her to the depth of the betrayal and the weight of his determination.

Camila's overconfidence led her to prepare for life alone in a superficial way, never fully committing to any final plans. She went through the motions half-heartedly, always waiting for Nic to tell her he would give her another chance. Taking minimal steps to secure her future, she remained convinced their separation was temporary. This denial only added to the tension in their household as Nic continued to move forward with his plans.

Faced with the reality of losing him, Camila was struck by the depth of her feelings. The changes she saw in Nic made her realize she still loved him, and their shared history wasn't something she could easily discard. She regretted underestimating his resolve and now felt desperate to fight for her family.

Nic moved forward with newfound confidence, assertive and independent, no longer consulting her on matters involving the children or household. Camila found herself drawn to his new resolve, no longer seeing him as weak. When he had treated her as an equal, consulting her on major issues, she had been irritated, viewing it as weakness. She had misinterpreted his kind and respectful demeanor. Now, seeing him take charge and move forward without her, she realized with painful clarity just how profoundly she had misunderstood and taken him for granted. She admired his strength and resolve, lamenting that it was now too late to give him the respect he had always deserved.

She noticed how his eyes sparkled when he returned from seeing friends and the faint smile he carried, as if holding a secret for the first time in years. With each passing day, it became clearer that she didn't want to lose him. She began to notice the small details about Nic—the way he laughed, the way he carried himself with newfound confidence. She remembered the man she had fallen in love with years ago and, for the first time in a long time, wanted to fight for their relationship.

Camila attempted to reconnect by spending more time with Nic and the children, asking about his day, and offering to help with tasks she had long ignored. She cooked, cleaned, and volunteered to handle the carpool, seeming to overcompensate. But every attempt to bridge the gap seemed to push him further away, leaving her questioning her worth and decisions. She was torn between the memory of her passionate affair with Marcos and the undeniable love she still felt for Nic. Her motivations were complex, rooted in a desire for validation, excitement, and escape from the mundane. Yet now, those very desires had led to profound regret.

One night, she found herself studying him from afar. Nic was engrossed in a book, the living room lamp casting a warm glow across his face. Without a word, Camila moved to the edge of the sofa, her presence disrupting the quiet atmosphere. His attention shifted from the book to her, his body tensing at her proximity.

Camila reached out, caressing his face, her fingers lingering on his skin. The gesture was unfamiliar, tentative, as if she were trying to remember how to touch him, how to connect. Her hand rested lightly against his cheek, the touch almost reverent, as though testing the boundaries of what remained between them.

Nic flinched at her touch, his jaw tightening. He felt repulsed by her presence but didn't want to cause a scene, fearing she might wake the children. He hoped his body language would convey his discomfort and that she would leave. The tension in his body was palpable, his grip on the book tightening as he fought to maintain composure.

Camila misinterpreted his flinch as hesitation rather than rejection. She convinced herself that his reaction signaled lingering feelings, a crack in his resolve. Hesitating briefly, her lips graced his with a tentative kiss. It was soft, careful, an attempt to bridge the growing distance between them, but the connection she sought wasn't there. His response was passive, void of emotion, and she felt the hollow space between them expand. The moment stretched into an uncomfortable pause, both frozen in the realization that their former intimacy had vanished. The restless detachment was undeniable. His lack of response acknowledged that their bond was broken beyond repair.

Nic, no longer able to hide his repulsion and disgust at her presence and attempts to seduce him, finally spoke, his voice low and strained. "Camila, please don't. It's too late for this. Your affair ended any potential for reconciliation. It's too little, too late."

Camila pulled away, feeling her failure settle heavily in her chest. She stood up, movements stiff with defeat, and retreated to her room. Nic remained on the sofa, staring blankly at his book. The atmosphere between them had grown colder and more distant, convincing her that she had lost him forever.

As she lay in bed, the weight of her choices pressed down. She had destroyed everything she once held dear. The realization that it was too little, too late, left her hollow. Redemption wouldn't come easily, but she was determined to try—for her children and perhaps, one day, for Nic's forgiveness.

He had loved her despite her flaws, but now he was choosing to move on without her, leaving her with nothing but regret. His words echoed in her mind: "Forgiveness is earned, not demanded." For the first time, she truly understood. Forgiveness might never come, but if there was even the smallest chance, she had to try.

Betrayal cuts deeper than any wound, especially from someone you trust. Nic's confrontation of Camila at the hotel was about reclaiming his dignity and shattering her illusion of hidden deception. Trust, once broken, is nearly impossible to restore. No amount of apologies or excuses can erase the hurt of betrayal.

Camila knew judgment would follow her, casting long shadows. But she couldn't control that. The only thing she could control was what she did next. For the first time, she acknowledged the gravity of her actions—not just to Nic, but to herself and their children. She had destroyed their family through selfish desires and lies, and now she had to pick up the pieces alone. Whether she could rebuild, whether redemption was possible, remained uncertain.

As she stared at the ceiling, Camila realized that redemption wouldn't come from grand gestures or apologies. It would come, if at all, from regaining her children's trust, day by day. The road ahead was long, uncertain, and lonely. But it was all she had left. She was determined to take it one day at a time, hoping to someday find peace—not in others' forgiveness, but in rebuilding her bond with Adrián and Celina.

Nic felt a strange sense of relief wash over him. Camila's attempt to reconnect only strengthened his resolve to move forward. He focused on building a stable, loving environment for their children, determined to give them the life they deserved. Each day brought new challenges, but also small victories that reinforced his purpose.

CHAPTER 14
BREAKING THE NEWS TO THE KIDS

A year after the dramatic confrontation, it was time for Camila to move out. She had found a small one-bedroom apartment five miles away, a stark contrast to the life they had built together. The hardest task lay ahead: breaking the news to Adrián and Celina. Nic had shielded the children from the turmoil that had plagued their parents' relationship, but now, they had to tell them the truth.

Nic and Camila sat down with their children at the kitchen table. Adrián and Celina sensed something serious was about to be discussed. Nic inhaled deeply, then spoke softly, "Adrián, Celina, your mom is going to be moving out."

The words hung in the air. For a moment, there was silence. Then, reality hit. Celina's eyes filled with tears as she clung to Nic, her small body shaking with sobs. Adrián's face crumpled as he tried to hold back tears, but they soon spilled over. He was angry and confused, while his sister was tearful and scared. Nic held them close, promising they would get through this together.

"Why?" six-year-old Celina cried, looking up at her parents. "Why is Mom leaving? Doesn't she love us anymore?"

Camila's voice trembled. "Oh no, sweetheart. Don't ever think that. Sometimes, grown-ups have problems they can't fix, no matter how hard they try. But we both love you very much, and that will never change."

Nine-year-old Adrián wiped his tears angrily. "This isn't fair! Why can't you just fix it?"

Nic hugged both children tightly, his heart breaking at their pain. "I know this is hard to understand, but we believe this is the best decision for everyone. We want you to be happy and feel safe."

The evening was filled with tears and questions. Nic and Camila did their best to comfort their children. The house, once a haven of warmth and laughter, now felt cold and alien. The remnants of happier times were everywhere—family photos, children's drawings, shared memories. Nic's mind swirled with emotions as he watched his children sleep, their faces tear-stained and innocent. The weight of the conversation lingered heavily in the air.

His thoughts were a storm of sadness, anger, and loss. He had loved Camila despite her flaws, but now he was letting her go, a decision that tore at him. He knew it was right, yet the pain was undeniable. As the night wore on, he gently stroked Adrián's hair, wishing things could have been different. Eventually, the exhaustion of the emotional conversation took its toll, and the children fell asleep, still clinging to their father. Nic gazed out the window, the night stretching endlessly before him, knowing the hardest part of their journey had just begun.

On the evening of May 30, 2013, Camila grabbed her bags, each step feeling like a weight pulling her deeper into the ground. Her heart ached with a complex mix of relief, regret, and sorrow. She had once believed she could have both—the thrill of Marcos and the stability of her family.

The reality of her choices was now harsh and unyielding. The judgment she feared from others felt insignificant compared to the judgment she cast upon herself. She realized that, in her quest for fulfillment, she had lost everything. As they broke the news to the children, Nic's eyes met hers, filled with a sadness that mirrored her own. Their children, too young to fully understand, clung to their father, their innocent faces etched with confusion as they absorbed the news.

Camila took a deep breath, the air heavy with the weight of finality. She stepped out into the night; the door closing softly behind her. The once familiar path now seemed foreign and daunting. She had to face the consequences of her actions alone, with only her memories to keep her company.

As she walked away from the life she had known, each step echoed the painful truth: in trying to have it all, she had ended up with nothing. The night was silent, save for the distant hum of the city, a stark contrast to the turmoil within her. She knew that the journey ahead would be long and difficult, but it was a path she had chosen, for better or worse.

Her mind a whirl of conflicting emotions. Would she ever find redemption? Could she rebuild her life? As she stepped into the cold night, the uncertainty of her future loomed. Each step reminded her of the life she had shattered, the family she had lost.

The next morning, the atmosphere was heavy with lingering emotions. Adrián and Celina sat at the kitchen table, picking at their breakfast. Nic watched them, his heart aching for their pain. Adrián broke the silence, "Dad, at first I was really upset that Mom was moving out. But then I thought about it. She's never home anyway, so it won't make much difference."

Nic felt a pang of sadness at his son's words. "I understand how you feel, Adrián. It's okay to be upset and hurt. But I promise you, things will get better. We'll make sure of it."

Celina looked up, her eyes red from crying. "Will we still see Mom?"

"Yes, sweetheart. You'll still see your mother. She'll always be your mom and will always love you. We'll work out times for you to spend with her."

Adrián nodded, thoughtful. "I just want things to be normal again."

Nic smiled gently. "We'll find a new normal. It might take time, but we'll get there. And we'll do it together."

The children took comfort in their father's words. Knowing they would stay in their home with him provided a sense of stability. The road ahead would be challenging, but Nic was determined to create a loving and supportive environment. He knew that with time, patience, and love, they would heal.

Nic fully embraced his role as a single father, ensuring his children thrived in a home filled with laughter and warmth. Yet, despite his resolve, there were moments of doubt. Late at night, when the house was quiet, he would lie awake, memories of happier times with Camila flooding his mind. He questioned whether he had made the right choices, the doubts gnawing at him in the darkness.

On her first day in the new apartment, Camila was struck by the emptiness that surrounded her. The walls, devoid of family photos, seemed to echo her loneliness. She missed her children intensely—their laughter, the bedtime stories, the simple joys of motherhood. The realization of what she had lost hit her hard. She hadn't wanted the divorce Nic had initiated; she had thought he would forgive her as he had before. But now, sitting alone, the reality of her situation was crushing. She had underestimated his resolve and overestimated her own ability to control the outcome.

Camila tried to fill the silence with activities. She unpacked boxes, arranged furniture, and attempted to create a sense of home. Yet, every corner of the apartment reminded her of the life she had left behind. She found herself longing for the chaos of family life, the constant noise, and the warmth that had once filled her home.

Amidst the unpacking, she placed the unsigned divorce papers on the kitchen table, staring at them with a mix of dread and hope. Nic had already signed them, but she couldn't bring herself to add her signature. Signing them would mean acknowledging the finality of their marriage, a reality she wasn't ready to accept. Deep down, she still harbored a faint hope that Nic might change his mind, although she knew this was unrealistic.

As she settled into the solitude, memories flooded back—Adrián's infectious giggle, Celina's curious questions, Nic's calming presence. Each memory was a painful reminder of what she had thrown away. She regretted not valuing what she had until it was gone.

In the quiet moments, Camila reflected on her actions and their impact. She realized she had taken Nic's forgiveness for granted, assuming he would always be there. Now, the depth of his determination and the finality of his decision left her feeling adrift. The weight of her choices pressed down on her, making it hard to breathe.

As they navigated their new lives apart, both Nic and Camila were forced to confront their own choices, the consequences that followed, and the uncertain path ahead. The journey to healing and self-discovery was just beginning, and the future was a blank canvas waiting to be painted with their decisions.

CHAPTER 15
GRANDPARENTS: PILLARS OF STRENGTH

Victoria and Daniel, affectionately known as Mama and Papa, were the bedrock of Nic's family. They weren't just the foundation; they were the unyielding strength and unwavering support upon which everyone leaned. They provided not only physical stability but also emotional resilience that held the family together, especially during the most challenging times.

Victoria, with her silver hair neatly tied back and her warm, twinkling eyes, had a way of making each grandchild feel special. Her children and grandchildren had endured her singing since birth, and they loved it. Each one had their own special song. She'd wake them up with a good morning song and put them to sleep with a goodnight song. She was a master storyteller, weaving tales of her own childhood adventures and imparting wisdom. Her hugs were like a warm blanket on a chilly day, offering comfort and security.

Daniel, with his gentle demeanor and infectious smile, perfectly complemented Victoria's vibrant energy. He had a knack for fixing things, whether it was a broken toy or a scraped knee. His patience was endless, and he took great joy in teaching his grandchildren how to fish, build birdhouses, and simply appreciate nature.

At the park, Daniel watched the children play, his eyes never leaving them. He was a helicopter Papa, always hovering, always protective, ensuring there were no accidents on his watch. When any of the children fell and scraped their knees, Papa was there in an instant, comforting and reassuring them.

"Papa, look! I can climb this!" Adrián called out.

"Be careful, buddy. I'm right here if you need me," Daniel replied, his heart swelling with pride.

Celina ran over, holding a flower. "Papa, this is for you!"

"Thank you, sweetheart. It's beautiful, just like you," Daniel said, kneeling down with a gentle smile.

During Nic and Camila's struggles, Mama and Papa were the constant stability the children needed. They increasingly took on the role of surrogate parents, caring for their grandchildren after school and on weekends. Each child had their own bedroom in Mama and Papa's home. They were playmates, role models, and mentors, teaching values, instilling ethnic heritage, and passing on family traditions.

Some of the children's fondest memories were of times spent with Mama and Papa. They played baseball, hide-and-seek, had picnics, and took trips to their favorite spots like McDonald's and Chick-fil-A, where they'd get takeout, park the SUV, and have an impromptu picnic by opening the trunk and sitting in the back. The kids loved this way more than eating at home.

Victoria stepped in to help with homework, organizing the children around the dining table and turning a stressful situation into a productive and enjoyable one. Her calm demeanor and structured approach provided the stability they needed.

Victoria and Daniel were immigrants from the Dominican Republic who grew up in New York—Victoria in Manhattan and Daniel in the Bronx. Victoria, the eldest of five, inherited her mother's nurturing nature and her father's resilience. She believed in the power of family and balanced discipline with affection.

Daniel, the youngest of three, was a serious and studious young man. He majored in business at New York University and worked for a major oil company in the city. Victoria and Daniel met at a neighborhood block party and, after a three-year courtship, married in New York. They had three children, with Nic being the oldest.

In 1990, Daniel's company moved its headquarters, and the family relocated to Fairfax, Virginia. Nic, then ten years old, was raised in Virginia. Daniel was a patient and understanding husband and father, the kind of grandfather who would spend hours helping with homework or building model airplanes. His protective nature stemmed from a deep-seated belief in the importance of a safe and loving environment for children to thrive.

One evening, as Nic sat at the kitchen table, Victoria joined him with a cup of tea. "Nic, can we talk for a minute?" she asked, her eyes filled with love and concern.

"Sure, Mama. What's on your mind?" he replied, sensing the seriousness in her tone.

She took a deep breath. "You know, your grandfather struggled with alcoholism. Most of his brothers did, too. It tore our family apart in ways you can't imagine."

Nic's hands trembled slightly. "I know, Mama. I remember the stories."

Victoria reached out, placing her hand over his. "I don't want that for you, Nic. I don't want that for your children. They look up to you. You are their hero. They depend on you for their protection. How would you feel if something happened to them while you were drunk or blacked out and couldn't protect them?"

His eyes filled with tears. "I never thought about it that way."

She squeezed his hand gently. "You owe it to them to be present, to be the father they need. You can break this cycle. I believe in you."

He nodded, the weight of her words sinking in.

When Nic announced he had stopped drinking, Victoria was ecstatic. She made sure their home was a haven, free from any temptations. Family dinners became a celebration of Nic's sobriety, with Victoria always finding ways to encourage him. She prepared delicious non-alcoholic drinks and toasted to Nic's strength and commitment.

Nic often reflected on his parents' unwavering support during his darkest nights. Their presence was a lifeline—never judging, always offering a steady hand and a listening ear.

One particularly difficult evening, Nic had purchased a bottle of liquor and set it on the table. He stared at it, his mind battling the overwhelming temptation to drink. His fingers drummed on the table, the ticking of the clock amplifying the tension in the room. Alone with his thoughts while the children and Camila slept, the urge to escape his pain through alcohol was almost unbearable.

Just as he was about to give in, his phone rang. It was his mother.

"Nic, I just wanted to check in on you."

Nic was astonished at her timing. It was almost as if she knew he needed her. "I'm fine, Mama," he said, his voice strained.

"You sound a bit stressed. Is everything okay?" she asked, her tone gentle yet probing.

"Yes, everything is fine," he replied, not wanting to admit he was about to reach for the bottle.

"Glad to hear. Remember, you're stronger than this addiction. You can overcome it. You have come so far, and both Papa and I are so proud of your accomplishments and how your recovery is progressing. Don't let any one moment define you."

Her words were a beacon of hope, cutting through the haze of his struggle. Nic's hand hovered over the bottle, trembling, before he finally pulled it back. After the call ended, he opened the bottle and poured it out, feeling a sense of relief wash over him. He went up to bed, grateful for the love and support that had saved him once again.

Camila watched from the sidelines, her heart heavy with mixed emotions. She couldn't deny the love and stability Victoria and Daniel provided for the children, but it also highlighted her own shortcomings. She felt a pang every time the children ran to their grandparents with open arms, their faces lighting up with joy. In contrast, they were hesitant during her visits.

She remembered the countless times she had tried to connect with the children, but her efforts always seemed to fall short. The bond Victoria and Daniel had with the children was something she had never achieved. It was a constant reminder of her failures as a mother.

Camila's feelings weren't just about the children's affection for their grandparents but also about the support Nic received. She felt isolated and alone, struggling to find her place in a family that seemed to function perfectly without her.

One evening, Camila sat alone in the living room, the house quiet except for the distant sound of the children playing with their grandparents. She felt a deep sense of loneliness. Why can't I be the mother they need? Why do they always turn to Victoria and Daniel?

She remembered a recent attempt to bond with Adrián. "Adrián, do you want to bake cookies with me?"

Adrián looked up, indifferent. "No, Mama makes the best cookies. I want to wait for her."

Camila's heart sank. She forced a smile and nodded, but inside, she felt a sharp sting of rejection. I try so hard, but it's never enough. They don't see me the way they see their grandparents.

Camila often reflected on her role in the family. She felt like an outsider, watching as Nic and the children thrived under Victoria and Daniel's care. Her own parents remained distant, not by choice, but because of the miles between them. This separation made her feel even more isolated and ill-equipped to be the mother her children needed. She struggled with guilt over her past actions. Her sense of inadequacy had led her to make decisions that strained her relationship with Nic and the children. She regretted the times she had lashed out in frustration, the moments when her insecurities had gotten the better of her. She had even criticized Victoria in front of the children, only to be told to stop.

Despite her struggles, Camila was determined to change. She wanted to be a better mother and partner. She started seeking ways to connect with her children, even if it meant taking small steps. One afternoon, she decided to join the children and Daniel at the park.

"Mind if I join you guys?" she asked.

Daniel smiled warmly. "Of course not, Camila. The more, the merrier."

She watched Adrián and Celina play, feeling a glimmer of hope. She knew it would take time, but she was willing to put in the effort. I can do this. I can be the mother they need. I just have to keep trying.

Victoria had always been sensitive to the energies around her. Every time she stepped into Nic and Camila's house, she felt an inexplicable heaviness—the kind that settles in the corners, making the air thick and dark. It was as if the walls themselves harbored negativity, and sunlight couldn't penetrate the gloom. The rooms seemed dim, and a sense of unease lingered. The energy was palpable, an invisible weight hovering in the air. Only those attuned to such atmospheres could sense the subtle, almost imperceptible tension that permeated the space.

During one of those visits, she noticed Nic sitting on the couch, staring blankly at the TV, his usual spark missing. "Nic, are you okay? You seem... different."

Nic shrugged, his eyes not meeting hers. "Just tired, Mama. It's been a rough few weeks."

Victoria glanced at Camila in the kitchen, her movements tense and hurried, the air between them crackling with unspoken tension. This house feels like it's suffocating under the weight of their struggles, she thought.

The first time Victoria visited Nic's house after the divorce, the transformation was striking. The air felt lighter, the rooms brighter. Nic greeted her with a genuine smile, a stark contrast to his previous demeanor.

"Hey, Mama. It's good to see you."

Victoria looked around, noticing the sunlight streaming through the windows, filling the house with warmth. "Nic, the house feels so different. It's like a dark cloud has lifted."

Nic nodded, relief evident in his expression. "Yeah, it feels like a weight has been lifted off my shoulders."

Victoria walked through the house, feeling the positive energy permeating the air. The unresolved issues and emotional turmoil had seeped into the very walls of this home. With Camila's departure, the negativity had dissipated, allowing peace to return.

Later, Victoria sat with Nic in the kitchen, a cup of tea in her hands. "Nic, this experience has validated my belief that our emotions and relationships deeply influence the energy in our environment."

Nic looked at his mother, curious. "What do you mean?"

"The atmosphere in a home can absorb and reflect the feelings of the people living in it. When there's tension, anger, or sadness, it can create a heavy, oppressive feeling. But when there's love, peace, and positivity, it feels lighter and more welcoming. The energy you put into your relationships and surroundings shapes the environment around you."

Nic leaned forward, intrigued. "So, the way we feel and interact with each other can change how a place feels?"

"Exactly," Victoria replied with a nod. "Your unresolved issues and emotional turmoil with Camila had created an oppressive atmosphere here. But now, with that tension gone, the house feels like a sanctuary again. It's a reminder that sometimes, change is necessary to restore balance and well-being."

Nic nodded, understanding dawning on his face. "You're right, Mama. It's like the house can finally breathe again."

As grandparents, Victoria and Daniel had a profound and nurturing impact on their grandchildren's lives. Nic fostered strong relationships between the generations, building bonds of love and friendship. The connection was mutual—grandparents needed their children and grandchildren just as much as they were needed. This interdependence created deep satisfaction and ensured that love and care flowed between generations.

Nic's children found unique acceptance and joy in their relationships with Victoria and Daniel. The grandparents served as stress buffers, family watchdogs, roots, arbitrators, and supporters, playing multiple essential roles in their lives.

The love and nurturing provided by Mama and Papa offered a safe harbor for the children during a time of extreme turmoil in their parents' lives. The bonds formed between the grandparents and their grandchildren were vital to the health and happiness of the family. Like a strong tree, the foundation and roots grounded them, the branches supported them, and the leaves provided shelter. In their embrace, each generation found the strength to grow and thrive.

Victoria and Daniel provided a sanctuary for Adrián and Celina, a place where love and stability were constants. Their home was filled with warmth, laughter, and cherished memories as they guided their grandchildren with gentle hands and open hearts. Their unwavering support and presence were pillars of strength, not only for the children but for Nic as well.

CHAPTER 16

THE OUTSIDER—THE BLAME GAME

Camila's days were haunted by a sense of loss. She constantly dwelled on what she had squandered—the love of her life, the trust of her family, and the simple joys of being part of her children's world. The suburban life that once suffocated her now seemed like a distant dream she could never reclaim.

Every time Camila tried to reconnect with her children, she encountered an invisible barrier. She didn't know their friends, their friends' parents, or the intricate web of relationships that formed their social lives. She missed out on the camaraderie of post-game gatherings, the shared laughter, and the sense of community that Nic had seamlessly integrated into.

Camila's attempts to reconnect often felt awkward and strained. She didn't know their favorite foods, hobbies, or the names of their best friends. The small details that made up their lives remained a mystery to her, and this realization cut deep.

Nic, on the other hand, had become a beloved figure in the community. Known as the dedicated single Dad, he received invitations to every event, from school plays to weekend barbecues. His presence served as a constant reminder of the life Camila had lost.

Camila's attempts to break through the barrier met with polite indifference. She attended school events and tried to engage with other parents, but the connections felt forced and superficial. The other parents, loyal to Nic and wary of Camila's past behavior, kept her at arm's length. They shunned her, not out of malice, but out of a protective instinct for their community and their friend. This exclusion cut deeply. Camila yearned to be part of her children's lives, to share in their triumphs and support them through their struggles. But no matter how hard she tried, she couldn't pierce the veil that separated her from the world she once took for granted.

The most painful part of Camila's regret was her estrangement from her children. She watched from the sidelines as Nic cheered them on at sporting events, attended parent-teacher conferences, and hosted sleepovers. Her children had grown accustomed to her absence. They loved her, but their bond with Nic was stronger, forged through years of his unwavering presence.

As the sun set, casting a warm glow over the neighborhood, Camila stood nervously on Nic's front porch. She hesitated before knocking, and when Nic opened the door, his surprise was evident.

"Camila? What are you doing here?" he asked, taken aback.

"Hi, Nic. I... I needed to talk to you. Can we sit down for a moment?" she replied, her voice uncertain.

"Sure. Come in," Nic said hesitantly.

They moved to the living room. Nic sat on the couch, and Camila took a seat across from him, fidgeting with her hands. Taking a deep breath, she began, "I've been doing a lot of thinking lately. About everything. The kids, us, my mistakes."

"Go on," Nic nodded.

"I know I've hurt you and the kids. I blamed you for my behavior, for my partying, but the truth is, I made those choices. I let my addictions control me," Camila said, her voice trembling.

Nic's thoughts raced. Yeah, don't forget about the affair. This is about the children, not me, so I'll let it go, but she just glossed over that part like it didn't happen.

"We both made mistakes, Camila. My drinking didn't help. But I stopped because I knew the kids needed me to be better," Nic responded quietly.

Tears welled in Camila's eyes. "And I promised to change too, but I didn't. I kept going out, doing drugs, neglecting our family. I failed you all."

"It wasn't easy for any of us. I wanted to support you, but I couldn't keep being the only one trying. The kids needed stability, and I had to move on," Nic replied with resignation.

"I understand that now. I see how much I've lost, and it's tearing me apart. I want to make things right, Nic. I want to be a better mother to Adrián and Celina," Camila said through her tears.

Nic's expression softened as he looked at her. "It's going to be a long road, Camila. They're hurt and confused, and it will take time for them to trust you again."

"I'm willing to do the work. I just need to know that I have your support, even if it's from a distance," Camila said with determination.

"I'll support you, but you need to take the lead. Show them through your actions that you've changed. That's the only way," Nic replied.

"Thank you, Nic. I won't let you down this time. I promise," Camila said, wiping her tears.

"Camila, this isn't about letting me down. For their sake, I hope you mean it because this time, you will be letting them down if you don't follow through," Nic replied firmly.

The week following her declaration to do better, Nic sat on the couch, looking through old family photos. The door opened, and Camila arrived to pick up the children for a scheduled visit, three hours late.

"Camila, we need to talk," Nic said firmly, looking up.

Camila sighed, rolling her eyes. "What now, Nic? I'm just here to pick up the kids."

"You're three hours late, and they're already settled for the night. I'm not waking them up. Even if they were awake, I wouldn't let you take them. You don't look sober. Have you been drinking?"

"Whether I've been drinking or not is none of your business. I'm here, aren't I? What more do you want? Nothing is ever good enough for you," Camila snapped. "I'm trying to make things right," she added defensively.

"It is my business because we're talking about our children's welfare. You may not care about their safety, but I do. Showing up late and in this condition isn't making things right, Camila. You can't just waltz in here anytime you want and pretend everything is fine," Nic's frustration resonated in his voice. "You were absent for years, Camila. You left me to be both mother and father to Adrián and Celina. You're still an absent parent. How do you expect them to trust you when you can't even honor a time commitment?"

"Nic, I had my reasons for my past behavior! You don't understand the pressure I was under," Camila raised her voice, tears threatening to spill.

"Pressure? What pressure, Camila? You never took on any real responsibility," Nic challenged, his tone unwavering.

"Maybe pressure isn't the right word. The point is that I was going through a lot of emotional issues trying to find my way. It was a time in my life when I felt lost and didn't know what I wanted. Maybe that was selfish, but it's the truth."

"Look, Camila, you can't blame being an absent mother on your emotional issues. When you're a parent, the children's welfare takes priority."

"I know that, Nic. But facing my family with all this is incredibly hard. They don't even know we've separated. In our Dominican culture, a mother losing custody is unheard of. They'll think I'm a terrible mother. I haven't told them about the divorce and custody because I fear their judgment," Camila sobbed.

"I understand it's hard, Camila. But this isn't about what others think. This is about our children. They need stability and a parent who is present and responsible," Nic's tone softened slightly.

"I'm aware I've messed up, Nic. But I want to be there for them now. I want to make amends," Camila said, her voice breaking.

"It's not that simple. You can't just erase the past. Adrián and Celina are hurt. It's going to take time for them to trust you again. You need to show them, not just tell them, that you've changed," Nic sighed.

"I know. But how do I start?" Camila asked, her voice small.

"Start by being honest with yourself, with them, and with your family. Accept responsibility for your actions. And most importantly, be consistent. They need to see you're committed to being a better mother," Nic said, looking her in the eyes.

"I'll try, Nic. I really will," Camila promised, wiping her tears.

"That's all I can ask for. But remember, it's a long road. Don't expect things to change overnight. Be patient with them," Nic said gently.

"I will be. Thank you, Nic," Camila replied with determination.

"For the kids' sake, I hope you mean it," Nic said quietly.

As Camila left, Nic watched her go with skepticism. She had made countless promises before, all of them hollow.

A month later, Camila was still struggling to bond with Adrián and Celina and wanted to talk to Nic for advice. One evening, when she was returning the kids from a weekend visit, she took a deep breath and approached him. The aroma of a simmering stew filled the kitchen as Nic stood at the counter, chopping vegetables with practiced ease. The rhythmic sound of the knife hitting the cutting board was the only noise until Camila's anxious voice broke the silence.

"Nic, I need to talk to you about the kids," she began, her voice trembling. "They still won't open up to me, and I feel you and your mother are poisoning them against me."

Nic sighed deeply, setting the knife down and turning to face her. "Camila, we've been over this. No one is poisoning the kids against you. They're hurt and confused, and it's going to take time for them to trust you again."

"You need to stop this paranoid thinking and recognize that my parents have been with those kids since the day they were born," he continued. "They've been surrogate parents when you and I were struggling with our personal issues. The children have always been close to their grandparents, who have been a constant presence in their lives, especially when you were preoccupied with work or social commitments. Their grandparents' home is a second home to them, filled with warmth and love."

Camila sat on a stool, gripping the edge tightly as she recalled how her children ran into Nic's parents' house, their laughter echoing down the quiet suburban street. A pang of insecurity and frustration hit her as she watched how happy they were to see their grandparents, hugging them tightly. They never gave her that kind of reception, and she felt like an outsider in her own family.

By the time Camila noticed the change in her children's behavior, it was too late. She began to see how her absence and indifference had affected them. She remembered the times she had missed their school events, the nights she had come home late, too tired to spend time with them. They had grown distant, preferring to spend time with their grandparents rather than her. As she stood in Nic's kitchen, the memory of a past confrontation with him flooded back.

"They don't want to be around me anymore," Camila had said, tears streaming down her face. "Your mother is turning them against me."

Nic had sighed, rubbing his temples. "Camila, it's not like that. They love spending time with her because she's always there for them."

"And I'm not?" Camila had shot back. "I'm their mother, Nic. They should want to be with me."

Nic's expression had softened slightly. "It's not about you not being their mother. It's about consistency. They need stability, and my mother provides that."

Camila's frustration had grown. "But every time I try to talk to them, they shut me out. I need your help to fix this," she had pleaded, her voice edged with desperation.

Back in the present, Camila's voice trembled. "I remember that argument so clearly. I felt so helpless then, and I still do now."

Nic's expression hardened as he spoke firmly. "Camila, I want to be supportive of your efforts to turn your life around, but it's not my responsibility to fix your relationship with the kids. That's something you need to work on directly with them."

Tears welled up in Camila's eyes. "I don't know how to reach them, Nic. They won't listen to me. They ignore me, not looking up from their phones. They don't take me seriously. It's like I don't exist."

Softening his tone, Nic stepped closer. "I understand it's hard, but you need to communicate with them directly. They need to hear from you, not through me or anyone else."

"Can't you at least talk to them for me?" she pleaded. "Help them understand that I'm trying?"

Nic shook his head, his resolve unwavering. "No, Camila. I can't be the go-between. It's important that you build that trust with them yourself. They need to see that you're committed to being a better mother."

Anger flashed in Camila's eyes. "So you're just going to leave me to figure this out on my own?"

"I'm not leaving you to figure it out alone," Nic replied calmly. "I'm here to support you, but you need to take responsibility for your actions and their consequences. It's the only way the kids will start to trust and respect you again."

Camila's shoulders slumped as she began to sob. "I just feel so lost, Nic. I don't know what to do."

Gently, Nic placed a hand on her shoulder. "Start by being honest with them. Apologize for the past and show them through your actions that you've changed. It's going to take time, but it's the only way."

Camila nodded, determination replacing her tears. "Okay. I'll try. But please, don't shut me out completely."

"I won't, Camila," Nic said softly. "But you need to meet us half-way. The kids need to see that you're serious about this."

"I will," Camila promised. "I'll start by being honest with them and letting them know what's going on."

Nic wrestled with the delicate balance of supporting Camila while enforcing the boundaries they both desperately needed. He knew that for her to rebuild trust with their children, she had to take responsibility for her actions and communicate directly with them. Yet, her erratic behavior often left him feeling as though he was managing three children instead of two. The weight of this responsibility pressed heavily on him as he navigated the fine line between being supportive and maintaining their family's fragile stability.

Despite the challenges, Nic remained resolute. He knew that for the sake of Adrián and Celina, he had to maintain a stable and loving environment. His commitment to his children gave him the strength to face each day, even as he dealt with the complexities of their family dynamics. As he closed the door behind Camila, he silently vowed to keep moving forward, one step at a time, for their future.

CHAPTER 17
CAMILA BREAKS HER SILENCE

Camila had finally mustered the courage to face her family and reveal the truth about her divorce. For six long months, they had been in the dark, unaware that she and Nic had separated, and that Nic had custody of their children. The thought of facing their disappointment and questions weighed heavily on her, but she knew it was time to face the consequences of her actions and begin the path to healing.

In the modest home filled with family photos and mementos, Camila's mother, Andrea, and her sisters, Isabella and Angela, sat gathered in the living room. Camila entered, visibly nervous, her heart pounding in her chest as she approached them, each step feeling like a march toward her own execution.

"Camila, mija, it's good to see you. Come, sit with us," Andrea said warmly, patting the seat next to her. "We haven't seen you in so long. When was the last time you visited?"

"It's been about seven months since she was here for my birthday," Angela said.

Camila sat down, her hands trembling slightly. Isabella noticed her tension immediately. "Camila, you seem really upset. What's going on?"

Taking a deep breath, Camila tried to steady herself. "My absence is partly why I wanted to talk to you. I need to tell you all something important."

Angela leaned forward, her brow furrowed with concern. "What is it? You know you can tell us anything."

"It's more of a confession. It's about Nic and the kids... and the divorce," Camila said, her voice barely above a whisper. She spoon-fed the confession, not wanting to shock them by revealing it all at once, deliberately letting out one detail at a time.

Andrea's smile faded, replaced by a frown. "Divorce? You never mentioned anything about a divorce. When did this happen?"

Tears welled up in Camila's eyes. "About six months ago. I didn't want to tell you because... because I was afraid of being judged."

Andrea's jaw dropped, "Six months? Mija, why would we judge you? Many relationships don't work out, and people go their separate ways," Andrea said, her voice gentle and comforting.

"Because Nic got custody of the kids," Camila whispered.

"Hold on—did you just say Nic has custody of the children?" Angela demanded.

Andrea's expression hardened. "Camila, what happened? Why did Nic get custody?"

Sobbing, Camila confessed, "I wasn't there for them. I was too caught up in my own life—partying, drinking, doing drugs. Nic had to be both mother and father to Adrián and Celina. I failed them."

Angela's eyes flashed with anger. "How could you, Camila? Those children needed you!"

Isabella shook her head, disappointment etched on her face. "We trusted you to care for your family. How could you let this happen?"

Andrea softened her tone, reaching for Camila's hand. "Camila, mija, we all make mistakes. But you need to take responsibility for your actions. Blaming others won't help."

"I know, Mamá. I know I messed up. But I want to make things right. I want to be a better mother," Camila cried, her voice breaking.

"It won't be easy. The children will need time to trust you again. And you need to show them that you've changed, not just tell them," Andrea said, her grip firm but gentle.

Angela nodded, her expression softening slightly. "Actions speak louder than words, Camila. You need to prove you're committed to being a better mother."

Isabella's eyes softened. "We're here for you, Camila. But you need to take the first step."

"I know all of this. I've had this same conversation with Nic, and he's said the same things. I promised him, just as I promise you, that I'll do whatever it takes to make things right," Camila said determinedly, wiping her tears

Andrea pulled her into a hug. "We believe in you, mija. But remember, it's a long road ahead. Stay strong and stay committed."

"There's one more thing I need to tell you if I'm going to be completely honest."

"You mean there's more?" Isabella asked, her voice tinged with disbelief.

"Yes, and it's the main reason Nic filed for divorce. As bad as being an absent mother and wife was, this is worse."

"¡Ay, Dios mío, Camila, what did you do?" Andrea's voice was filled with dread.

"Mamá, this won't be easy for me to confess, but I need to tell you everything."

Andrea, with her heart in her throat and voice shaking, said, "Go ahead, we're listening."

Camila sat across from her mother and sisters, her eyes filled with regret. "I had an affair with a man named Marcos Medina. He's a thirty-eight-year-old corporate lawyer. It was a terrible mistake," she confessed, her voice trembling. Camila took a deep breath, her eyes filled with a mix of fear and regret. She knew this moment would change everything. The room seemed to close in around them as Camila confessed the affair, each word heavy with the weight of her actions.

"Mamá, I met Marcos at a charity event hosted by his law firm. I felt neglected and unappreciated in my marriage, and his attention was flattering. Our conversations started light and flirtatious but quickly turned into a passionate affair. Marcos made me feel intensely alive, something I hadn't felt in my marriage to Nic. We would meet in secret, finding solace in each other's company.

"The affair created a deep rift between Nic and me. At home, I felt irritable and bored, no longer enjoying family time. Nic's stability and love felt like a burden, and I began to see him as an obstacle to the life I thought I wanted.

"Marcos knew our relationship was built on secrecy and deceit. He struggled with guilt, especially knowing I had a family. But his desire for me and the escape I provided were too strong to resist. As time went on, he became increasingly conflicted. He cared deeply for me, but he knew our relationship couldn't last as it was. Either I left Nic and the children, or I'd break up with him. Marcos didn't want to deal with children."

"¡Dios mío, Camila! How could you gamble your family's future for a man who wouldn't accept your children?" her mother said, shocked.

"That's not even the worst part."

"I can't believe this gets any worse," Angela said, her voice rising.

"The worst part is that Nic followed me one evening and confronted us in the hotel," Camila concluded, her voice breaking.

Andrea's face paled as she absorbed Camila's words. She took a deep breath, her eyes filled with a mix of disappointment and sorrow. "Oh, Camila," she whispered, shaking her head. "How could you let it get this far? I raised you better than this." Her voice trembled with emotion, but she reached out and took Camila's hand. "We all make mistakes, mija. But you need to understand the gravity of what you've done. It's not just about you; it's about your family, your children. You have to find a way to make this right."

Isabella sat in stunned silence, her eyes wide with disbelief. "I can't believe this," she finally said, her voice barely above a whisper. "You had everything, Camila. A loving husband, beautiful children... How could you throw it all away for some fling?" Her tone was harsh, but there was a hint of sadness in her eyes. "I don't even know who you are anymore." She stood up, pacing the room. "You need to fix this, Camila. For your kids, if nothing else. They deserve better."

Angela, finally finding her voice, said, "My God, my heart aches for Nic. He is such a good man, husband, and Dad. He didn't deserve this from you. I know he is hurting, and all I want to do is give him a hug. You are lucky he is not a violent man, and you are still alive to tell the story. Few men would have reacted with the composure he has. This could have ended in disaster for all involved. Thank your lucky stars that Nic is the kind of man he is. It takes strength and self-control to face this type of betrayal and not act out violently."

Andrea chimed in, "I agree with Angela. What I have always admired most about Nic is that he has always been a pillar of patience and understanding. Even in the face of such a profound betrayal, he chose to handle the situation with dignity. It's a rare quality, Camila. Many men would have let their anger control them. But Nic—he stood firm, not letting his emotions dictate his actions. He thought about the children, about protecting them from further hurt. It takes a truly remarkable person to prioritize love and protection over vengeance.

That's the kind of man Nic is. And you are incredibly fortunate that he is the father of your children."

Andrea's words hung in the air, each family member absorbing the gravity of what had been shared. Camila felt the weight of their disappointment, but also their love. She knew the road ahead would be long and arduous, but with their support, she believed she could begin to make amends.

"We're here for you, Camila," Andrea continued softly. "But you have to take the first step. It's up to you to rebuild what's been broken."

Camila nodded, determination setting in. "I will, Mamá. I promise. I'll do whatever it takes to make things right."

Her family's support, though tinged with disappointment, was the foundation she needed to start the difficult journey of healing and redemption. For the first time in months, she felt a glimmer of hope. They were all emotionally drained after Camila's confession. As they called it a night, each family member needed time to process what they had just heard, unable to believe how well Camila had kept her struggles hidden from them. She had maintained a perfect facade, concealing the turmoil that had torn her life apart.

The next day, in Andrea's kitchen, a warm and familiar space filled with the aroma of home-cooked food, Andrea was preparing dinner when Camila entered, seeking comfort. The kitchen, with its worn wooden table and the scent of simmering stew, had always been a place of solace for Camila.

"Mamá, I don't know what to do. I feel like everything is falling apart," Camila said, sinking into a chair at the kitchen table, her shoulders slumped. The weight of her confession still hung heavily on her.

Andrea sighed, stirring a pot on the stove. She glanced at Camila, her heart aching for her daughter. "Camila, mija, I know you're struggling. But you need to understand that your actions have consequences." Her voice was gentle but firm, a mix of love and disappointment.

Tears filled Camila's eyes, her voice breaking. "I know, Mamá. I just need your support right now." She felt like a child again, seeking comfort in her mother's presence.

Andrea paused, her hands trembling slightly as she set the spoon down. She turned to face Camila, her expression torn. "I want to support you, Camila. You're my daughter, and I love you. But I can't ignore what you've done." The pain in her eyes was evident, a reflection of the betrayal she felt.

"Please, Mamá. I need you," Camila pleaded, her voice desperate. She felt the walls closing in, the reality of her actions suffocating her.

Andrea walked over and sat down next to Camila, taking her hand. "I know, mija. But you need to take responsibility for your actions," she said softly, her voice filled with both love and firmness. Internally, she reminded herself, Stay strong, Andrea. She needs tough love right now.

"I'm trying, Mamá," Camila sobbed, her tears falling onto the table. The guilt and shame were overwhelming, but she knew she had to face them.

Andrea squeezed her hand gently. "I believe you, Camila. But believing isn't enough. You need to show it through your actions," she said, her voice firm yet gentle. She knew this was the only way Camila could truly begin to heal.

Camila nodded, tears streaming down her face. "I will, Mamá. I promise." She felt a flicker of hope, a small light in the darkness.

Andrea pulled her daughter into a tight hug. "I know you can do it. But remember, it's a long road," she whispered, her voice filled with both hope and caution. She prayed that Camila would find the strength to change.

After her confession to her family, Camila felt drained, yet a sense of relief washed over her. The deception had been a heavy weight to bear, and now, with everything out in the open, she could finally begin to heal. She sat quietly, feeling a mix of relief and exhaustion.

Her mind drifted to the times she had neglected her children—the look of disappointment in Adrián's eyes when she missed his soccer games, and Celina's tears when she wasn't there to tuck her in at night. These painful memories fueled her determination to make amends.

Camila also reflected on her relationship with Nic. She remembered the love and stability he had provided, the sacrifices he had made for their family. She had taken it all for granted, blinded by her own desires. The confrontation at the hotel had been a wake-up call, a moment of clarity that shattered her illusions. She recalled what had transpired that evening.

Nic had followed her, his suspicions finally confirmed. When he saw Camila with Marcos at the hotel, his heart shattered. He confronted them, his face a mask of pain and betrayal.

"Camila, how could you?" Nic's voice was low, trembling with emotion. "I trusted you. I loved you. How could you do this to our family?"

She had never seen him so broken. His eyes, usually so full of warmth and love, were now filled with hurt and anger. She tried to speak, but the words caught in her throat.

"Nic, I'm so sorry," she whispered, tears streaming down her face. "I never meant to hurt you."

Nic shook his head, his expression hardening. "Sorry isn't enough, Camila. You've destroyed everything we built together. Our family, our trust... it's all gone."

The confrontation had been a turning point. Nic's pain was palpable, and it forced Camila to confront the reality of her actions. She realized then that she had not only betrayed her husband but also shattered the foundation of their family.

As Camila sat in the kitchen, the warmth of her mother's embrace still lingering, she felt a glimmer of hope. Her family's support, despite their disappointment, gave her the strength to face the consequences of her actions and strive to rebuild her life. She knew the road ahead would be challenging, but for the first time in a long while, she felt a sense of purpose. Camila vowed to earn back the trust of her children and Nic. She would show them through her actions that she had changed. It wouldn't be easy, but she was ready to fight for her family and her future.

CHAPTER 18
A MOTHER'S EFFORTS TO RECONNECT

After visiting her family, Camila had her children for their first weekend visit since her confession. The living room, adorned with family photos, basked in the soft glow of afternoon sunlight. Fresh-baked cookies perfumed the air, mingling with lavender from a nearby candle. Adrián and Celina sat on the couch, lost in their smartphones. Camila entered carrying a tray of snacks, her smile wavering.

"Hey Adrián, Celina, can we talk for a minute?" Her voice carried a thread of hope.

Adrián glanced up briefly before returning to his phone. Celina didn't look up at all. Camila's chest tightened at their indifference, but she knew rebuilding trust would take time. Determined, she sat beside them, ready to begin the long journey toward redemption.

Later, alone in her bedroom, Camila finally let her tears fall. She lay on her bed, staring at the ceiling as doubts crowded her mind. Will they ever forgive me? Can I really make things right? The weight of her mistakes pressed against her chest, but her resolve held firm.

The pattern repeated during subsequent visits. She spent afternoons in the kitchen, the familiar clinking of pots and pans reminding her of happier times. She set the table with care, arranging their favorite snacks and drinks with precise attention.

When Adrián and Celina arrived, they barely acknowledged her presence. They sat at the table, absorbed in their phones, answering her attempts at conversation with single words. Yet Camila remained steady, asking about their days and interests. She noticed when Adrián's pasta needed more cheese and quietly added it. She remembered Celina's favorite dessert and served it without fanfare. Each small gesture became a wordless plea for connection.

As weeks passed and visits remained strained, Camila's dedication never wavered. She showed up consistently, attended school events, and offered homework help. One rainy afternoon, while helping Celina with a school project as Adrián watched TV, raindrops tapped a gentle rhythm against the windows. When Celina struggled with her assignment, she finally turned to Camila for help. Camila guided her daughter through each step, offering quiet encouragement.

After completing the project, Celina gave Camila a brief, tentative hug—the first show of affection in months. Camila's heart soared, but she contained her joy, afraid of overwhelming her daughter. She simply smiled and continued working. Adrián, watching the exchange, seemed to soften slightly. Though he remained silent, his defensive posture relaxed.

Camila understood her path to redemption would be long, but these small victories strengthened her commitment to rebuilding relationships with her children.

During another visit, Camila approached them. "Hey, kids. I brought some snacks. Thought we could spend some time together."

Adrián barely shifted. "Thanks. Just leave it there."

Celina glanced up briefly. "Yeah, thanks, Mom."

Camila settled beside them, trying to bridge the gulf between them. "How was school today? Anything interesting happen?"

"It was fine," Adrián mumbled, eyes fixed on his screen.

"Same as always," Celina added, still typing.

"I thought maybe we could play a board game or watch a movie together," Camila suggested.

Adrián exhaled sharply, his frustration breaking through. "Maybe later, Mom. I'm busy right now."

Celina nodded. "Yeah, maybe later."

Camila persisted despite the rejection. "I understand you're busy, but spending time with you matters to me."

Adrián looked up, pain flashing in his eyes. "Why now, Mom? You never cared before." His words cut deep, weighted with accumulated hurt.

Camila's heart clenched. "I know I failed you before, but I'm working to change that. I want to make things right."

Celina's voice softened. "It's just hard, Mom. We're not used to this."

"I understand that. I really do. But can we try? Just for a little while?" Camila asked.

Adrián set his phone down reluctantly. "Fine. But just for a bit."

Celina followed suit. "Okay, Mom. We'll try."

Camila smiled, acknowledging the distance that remained. "Thank you. That means everything to me."

As her children cautiously agreed to spend time with her, Camila felt hope flutter in her heart. She understood that rebuilding their relationship would be a long and challenging process, but she was ready to face it. Sitting beside them, she contemplated the difficult path forward. Each tiny step could lead toward healing, and she promised herself to remain steady and patient. For the first time in months, she felt truly purposeful. Camila silently vowed to do whatever it would take to earn back their trust and build deeper bonds with her children, knowing her actions—not her words—would determine her success.

Camila regretted not having bonded with her children when they were younger. She realized now that those formative years were crucial. Studies show that bonding with children during their early years fosters emotional security, social competence, and cognitive development. The strong parent-child bond provides a secure base for children to explore the world, build self-confidence, and develop healthy relationships in the future. As she reflected on these missed opportunities, Camila vowed to make the most of every moment moving forward, determined to provide the love and support her children needed to thrive.

She remained hopeful, as research showed that while early bonding is crucial, it's never too late to build a strong relationship. Studies suggest that consistent, positive interactions can help strengthen bonds even as children grow older. While early bonding has a significant impact, ongoing efforts to connect with children can still positively influence their social skills, emotional well-being, and resilience.

So, while the bond may not be exactly the same as it would have been if formed earlier, it is still possible to build a meaningful and supportive relationship with her children. Camila's dedication and consistent efforts could help bridge the gap and create a strong, loving connection with Adrián and Celina.

CHAPTER 19

A BREADTH OF FRESH AIR—LONG DISTANCE RELATIONSHIP

After years of enduring Camila's superficiality and being taken for granted, Nic finally decided to move on. Though painful, he realized he deserved someone who would appreciate him for who he was. He found solace in work and hobbies, gradually rebuilding his life.

Joining a local hiking group introduced him to people who shared his passion for nature and adventure. These new experiences helped him rediscover himself and brought a fulfillment he hadn't felt in years. On weekends when the children were visiting their mom, Nic took the opportunity to socialize and date people he met through his hiking group and other hobbies.

Slowly, Nic began to enjoy his newfound freedom and independence. He spent more time outdoors, exploring trails and mountains, and connecting with others who shared his interests. The camaraderie and shared experiences with his new friends provided a sense of belonging and support that he had been missing.

Nic's confidence grew as he embraced these new aspects of his life. The regular hikes, social gatherings, and time spent in nature helped him heal from the emotional wounds of his past. He started to see a future where he could be happy and fulfilled, surrounded by people who valued and respected him.

Through this journey, Nic discovered that moving on was not just about finding someone new, but about rediscovering himself and what made him truly happy. He realized that he didn't need to settle for less and that he deserved to be with someone who appreciated him fully. This newfound self-awareness and appreciation for his own worth gave Nic a sense of peace and contentment, allowing him to look forward to the future with hope and optimism.

During the summer of 2014, Nic took a much-needed vacation to Florida with his childhood friends. It was during this trip that he met the captivating Celia Lopez.

One balmy evening, at a beachside bar, he felt lighter than he had in years. He noticed Celia across the room, and their eyes met, sparking an instant connection. Encouraged by his friends, Nic approached her. They quickly discovered shared loves: travel, good music, and genuine conversation. Celia's infectious laughter drew Nic in, and he found himself captivated by her warmth and authentic interest in others

Celia Lopez had built her reputation as a freelance photographer, known for her stunning travel pieces. She had spent recent years documenting adventures around the world. Despite her professional success, she carried her own emotional scars. A recent long-term relationship had ended, leaving her questioning her choices and future. The beginning had been filled with excitement and shared dreams, but time revealed diverging paths. Her ex-partner craved stability while she yearned for adventure and new experiences. The breakup left her wondering if prioritizing her career had been misguided.

Her recent heartbreak made her cautious. She questioned whether her focus on career had cost her chances at lasting love, fearing her desire for independence might always clash with the need for commitment. Yet something about Nic felt different. His honesty and the way he spoke about his children with such devotion captivated her. Their conversation flowed effortlessly, and by evening's end, both felt an uncanny familiarity, as if they'd known each other far longer than mere hours.

Back in Virginia, Nic couldn't shake thoughts of Celia. Their connection had been unmistakable, and he eagerly anticipated their next encounter. Through texts and video calls, their bond deepened. Celia's vibrant spirit brought joy to Nic's life, and he found himself smiling more than he had in years.

Their conversations ranged from favorite travel destinations to deepest fears and dreams. They shared life stories, laughing and sometimes crying together. Nic opened up to Celia in ways he never had before; her understanding and empathy made him feel truly heard. Similarly, Celia treasured Nic's genuine interest in her life and unwavering support for her career.

Despite the physical distance, they nurtured their connection. They watched movies over video calls, exchanged surprise care packages, and made time for virtual date nights. Their constant communication built a foundation of trust and transparency. Nic admired Celia's creativity and resilience, while she respected his dedication to his children and his ability to balance life's demands.

As time passed, their bond strengthened. They shared future hopes, supporting each other's dreams while learning to navigate the challenges of a long-distance relationship. They found comfort in regular communication and small gestures of affection. Trust grew naturally, as did their ability to honor each other's boundaries and needs.

Gradually, the distance felt less daunting. Their relationship had developed enough strength to weather any challenge. They found peace knowing they were building something genuine and lasting, founded on mutual trust and open communication.

Though Nic's work and parental responsibilities made travel difficult, he managed to plan another trip to Florida two months later. Anticipation built with each call and message. Their reunion exceeded every hope. They spent the day exploring local sights, sharing stories, and savoring each other's company. The evening culminated in a beachside dinner, watching the sunset while discussing their shared future.

What began as a weekend getaway had transformed into something profound. Meeting Celia had rekindled Nic's hope, bringing happiness he'd forgotten was possible. For Celia, Nic proved that meaningful connections could emerge from unexpected moments.

Their relationship flourished through trust and honest communication. They championed each other's dreams, their bond growing stronger through shared experiences. Nic discovered that true relationship happiness came from being valued for his authentic self, not for what he could offer.

During a visit to Virginia, Celia sat at the kitchen table, staring at the offer letter from her company on her laptop. It was a dream promotion that promised to elevate her career, but it came with a catch: frequent travel and the possibility of relocating. Nic entered the room, sensing her turmoil.

"Hey, what's on your mind?" he asked, sitting beside her.

Celia sighed, running a hand through her hair. "I got the promotion. It's everything I've worked for, but it means a lot of travel. Maybe even moving."

Nic took her hand, his expression thoughtful. "That's amazing news, Celia. I'm so proud of you. Why the concerned look?"

"I don't want to disrupt what we have," Celia said, her voice trembling. "I love you and the kids. I want to be here as much as possible."

Nic squeezed her hand reassuringly. "We'll figure it out together. Maybe there's a way to make it work without sacrificing either your career or our family."

Over the next few weeks, they explored various options. Celia spoke with her employer about flexible work arrangements and considered the logistics of managing travel. She sought advice from mentors who had faced similar challenges. Finally, she made her decision. She accepted the promotion but negotiated a schedule that allowed her to work remotely part of the time and limit her travel. It wasn't easy, but it was a compromise that honored both her career aspirations and her commitment to her relationship with Nic.

As she shared the news with Nic and the children, Celia felt a sense of relief and excitement. She had found a way to pursue her dreams without losing sight of what mattered most. With Nic's unwavering support, she knew they could navigate any challenges that came their way.

Celia had built a successful career through self-motivation and fierce independence. She loved Nic and his children deeply, envisioning a future together. However, Nic's hesitation to commit to marriage weighed heavily on her. His experiences with Camila had made him cautious about entering another serious relationship.

Her relationship with Nic was the inverse of her previous one. Now, she was ready to settle down, while Nic held back. The physical and emotional distance between them posed a constant challenge. Living out of state, Celia struggled to maintain a close connection with Nic, especially given his reluctance to commit. Her need for reassurance often clashed with his cautious nature, creating tension between them.

Meeting Nic had been unexpected—a chance encounter that rekindled her hope. In her previous relationship, she had chosen her blossoming career over settling down. This time, she didn't want to sacrifice her relationship for her career. Celia's insecurities stemmed from Nic's reluctance to commit long-term. Despite their open communication, she often felt caught in a one-sided relationship, ready to commit while Nic held back. She found herself empathizing with her former partner, understanding how he must have felt when she wasn't ready to commit. This newfound perspective added to her inner turmoil.

Being on opposite ends, they frequently misunderstood each other's needs and intentions. Celia felt distant and unsupported, while Nic felt pressured and unsure. Through advice from friends and family, they both worked to find balance between Celia's need for emotional closeness and Nic's need for time and space. Through open communication and mutual support, they found a way to honor their individual dreams while building a future together. Their relationship grew stronger, built on trust and understanding.

Celia sank into her favorite armchair, the soft fabric embracing her. She gazed out the window, lost in thought. Her journey had been anything but easy. The scars from her past relationship lingered, casting shadows over her present with Nic. Moments of doubt and insecurity crept in, despite her efforts to move forward.

Later, perched on the edge of her bed, Celia gripped her phone like a lifeline. The day had been long and draining, and all she craved was the comfort of Nic's voice. But lately, their conversations carried unspoken tension. She took a deep breath and dialed his number, her heart racing.

"Hey, Nic," she said softly when he answered. "I miss you."

"I miss you too, Celia," Nic replied, his voice blending warmth with exhaustion. "It's been a long day."

"I know," Celia said, her voice trembling. "I just wish we could see each other more often. This distance is really hard."

Nic sighed heavily. "I know it's tough. But with the kids and my job, it's hard to find time to travel."

Celia swallowed hard, fighting back tears. "I understand, but I need more from you, Nic. I need to know that we're moving towards something, that there's a future for us."

A long, painful silence followed. "Celia, I care about you deeply, but I'm not ready to commit to marriage right now. My past with Camila... it still affects me."

Tears stung her eyes. "I get that, but I need reassurance. I need to know that I'm not just waiting for something that might never happen."

Nic's voice softened with a tenderness that made her heart ache. "I don't want to lose you, Celia. Let's talk about this more when I visit next weekend. We need to find a way to make this work for both of us."

After the call ended, Celia sat in silence, her emotions churning between hope and anxiety. She loved Nic and his children, but the uncertainty gnawed at her. They needed to bridge both the physical and emotional distance between them.

Determined to heal, Celia turned to self-reflection and therapy. With Nic's support, she confronted her fears head-on. Each therapy session peeled back layers of pain, revealing a stronger, more confident woman beneath. She began to see herself anew, ready to embrace the future.

Integrating into Nic's family presented its own challenges. The children, especially Adrián, were initially wary. Despite tense moments and misunderstandings, Celia remained patient and empathetic, knowing that trust would take time and consistent effort.

Gradually, her genuine care and engaging personality won the children over. She invested time in learning their interests and finding ways to connect. Even Adrián, the most resistant, eventually warmed to her. One day, he said, "I wish Mom was more like you, Celia."

Her heart swelled with emotion. She had always dreamed of being a mother, and Adrián's words felt like a dream realized. Through patience and love, she had found her place in Nic's life and in his children's hearts.

Together, they built a harmonious blended family, where love and understanding bridged the gaps of their past. Celia's personal growth and dedication to bonding with Nic's children strengthened their connections.

Nic sat alone on the porch, the evening's cool air contrasting with the day's warmth. He studied the old photo album in his hands, turning pages filled with memories of life with Camila. The smiles in the pictures echoed a simpler time before arguments and growing distance divided them. He paused at their wedding photo, taking in Camila's radiant smile and his hopeful expression. He remembered their promises and shared dreams, now faded into a reality far from what they had envisioned.

Closing the album, Nic sighed. The fear of repeating past mistakes weighed heavily on him. He didn't want to experience that same sense of loss and disappointment. With Celia, everything felt different. Her genuine warmth and understanding made him want to believe in love again, yet his scars held him back.

They shared activities like hiking and exploring nature, bringing joy and adventure back into Nic's life. These experiences created positive memories and helped him move forward. Celia's honesty fostered trust, contrasting sharply with his past relationship. Knowing he could rely on her made him feel secure and valued. She encouraged his passions and dreams, motivating him to explore new opportunities.

Through Celia, Nic learned that love could be nurturing, supportive, and built on mutual respect. This perspective helped him release the past and embrace a healthier view of relationships. Their deep connection proved instrumental in his healing, showing him that meaningful relationships were possible and that he deserved someone who truly valued him.

Despite this transformation, Nic hesitated to commit long-term. His trauma from Camila ran deep. Memories of betrayal and emotional scars haunted him, manifesting as relationship PTSD. He needed time to fully heal and rebuild trust. His approach to this new relationship required caution and care, giving himself space to restore his sense of security. His reluctance wasn't about his feelings for Celia, but rather a necessary step in his emotional recovery. He hoped she would grant him the patience and time needed to heal, trusting their bond would strengthen with time.

Nic's relationship with Celia was a transformative experience that helped him heal from the wounds of his past and find happiness and fulfillment in a new, supportive partnership. It was a testament to the power of genuine connection and the importance of being with someone who appreciates and respects you for who you are.

CHAPTER 20

THE NEW REALITY - MOVING ON AND FINDING CLOSURE

Camila paced back and forth in her living room, her mind racing with turmoil. She had heard through the grapevine that Nic had a new girlfriend. The thought of him moving on so quickly infuriated her. Despite her own affairs, she had always assumed Nic would pine for her, his beautiful ex-wife.

At a school event for their children, Camila's suspicions were confirmed. She watched as Nic arrived with a woman she didn't recognize. The woman was laughing, her hand resting casually on Nic's arm. Camila's heart sank, a mix of jealousy and indignation bubbling up inside her. A mutual friend noticed her staring and leaned in to whisper, "That's Nic's new girlfriend, Celia. They've been seeing each other for a few months now."

Camila felt a surge of anger. How could he move on so easily? The realization that Nic had found happiness with someone else stung deeply. She had always believed that he would be there, waiting for her, despite everything. The sight of Nic with Celia filled her with a sense of betrayal, as if her place in their shared history was being erased.

Later that evening, as the sun dipped below the horizon, Camila stood on Nic's front porch with a mix of determination and vulnerability. Her heart pounded as she struggled to mask her feelings of being replaced by Celia. Now, face-to-face with the man who had once been her everything, Camila felt a strange mix of anger and liberation, ready to unearth the truth and finally close this painful chapter. "Nic, we need to talk," she demanded, her voice trembling with rage.

Nic sighed, sensing the confrontation. "What is it, Camila?"

"Who is she?" Camila spat out. "Who is this woman you've been parading around?"

Nic took a deep breath, trying to stay calm. "Her name is Celia. We've been seeing each other for a while now."

"How could you?" Camila's voice cracked. "I never thought you'd move on so quickly."

Nic's patience was wearing thin. "Camila, you had your affairs. You moved on long before our marriage ended. Why is it so hard to accept that I'm doing the same?"

Camila was silent for a moment, the truth of Nic's words sinking in. She had always assumed he would be there, waiting for her, despite everything. "I just... I never thought you'd actually move on," she admitted, her voice softer now.

Nic's expression softened with empathy. "Camila, I'll always care about you. You're the mother of my children. But we both need to move forward. Holding onto the past isn't helping anyone, especially not the kids. They need us to show them that life goes on, that we can find happiness again. Our relationship has changed; we're no longer partners in life but co-parents. We need to set boundaries and respect each other's roles in the kids' lives. While we'll always be connected through them, our paths are separate now. It's time we both embrace that and focus on being the best parents we can be."

Camila took a deep breath, the initial wave of anger subsiding into a dull ache. She realized that this confrontation was not just about Celia, but about the unresolved feelings that still lingered between them. There were lingering regrets and what-ifs: the moments of connection they had shared before their relationship deteriorated, the dreams they had built together that were never realized, and the guilt and hurt that accompanied their betrayals. Both were still haunted by the memories of what could have been, struggling to fully let go and embrace their separate futures.

As they continued talking, Nic mentioned, "The kids and I are going on a mini-vacation this weekend."

"A vacation? Where to?" Camila's eyebrows shot up in surprise.

"We're going camping. And... well, Celia is coming with us," Nic hesitated before answering.

Shock and anger flashed across Camila's face. "Your girlfriend? And you're taking my children on a vacation with her?"

Remaining calm, Nic nodded. "Yes, Camila. The kids like her, and I think it will be good for them to spend some time together." Softening his tone, Nic stepped closer. "I understand this is hard for you, but the kids need stability and happiness. They deserve positive experiences, even if it means including Celia. I can't put my life on hold forever. I need to move on, too."

Camila's anger flared again. "Happiness? How can they be happy with someone else playing mom?" Her voice cracked with a mix of jealousy and desperation. "Do you really think she can take my place? Do you think she can love them the way I do? How can you be so sure she won't hurt them?"

Nic sighed, trying to maintain his composure. "Camila, no one is trying to replace you. Celia is just trying to be a positive presence in their lives. She's important to me, and she makes me happy."

Tears began to form in Camila's eyes as she choked out, "How can you say that? You're moving on with your life, and I'm still trying to fix mine. It's not fair."

Camila took a deep breath, the initial wave of anger subsiding into a dull ache. She realized that this confrontation was not just about Celia, but about the unresolved feelings that still lingered between them. "I feel like I have been cast away from my home and my family. This is not what I wanted. You forced the divorce on me, not giving me a choice as to what I wanted. I always thought our separation was temporary. I thought we'd find a way back to each other. Seeing how you feel about Celia... crushes any hope of reconciliation."

Nic's face softened with understanding but remained firm. "Camila, I understand how you feel, but the reality is that our relationship was broken long before Celia came into the picture. We both made mistakes, and we both have to live with the consequences. Forcing ourselves back into a relationship that wasn't working would only hurt us and the children more. Moving forward is the best thing we can do for ourselves and for them."

Nic's voice grew firm. "Camila, this isn't about replacing you. It's about giving the kids a sense of normalcy and joy. They need to see that life can still be good, even after everything that's happened."

Camila's shoulders slumped as she began to sob. "I just feel like I'm losing them, Nic. First, I lose you, and now my children are slipping away, too."

Gently, Nic placed a hand on her shoulder. "You're not losing them, Camila. But you need to accept that things have changed. The best thing you can do is to be there for them and show them that you're committed to being a better mother."

Wiping her tears, Camila nodded. "I'm trying, Nic. I really am. But it's so hard."

Nic nodded in understanding. "I know it is. But you have to keep trying. For their sake."

Taking a deep breath, Camila steadied herself. "Fine. But please, don't push me out of their lives completely."

Nic's voice softened further. "I won't, Camila. But you need to meet me halfway."

With a determined look, Camila promised, "I'll try. I promise."

As Camila drove away, her thoughts churned with a mix of emotions. She realized how deeply she had hoped for a reconciliation with Nic and seeing him genuinely happy with Celia stung more than she had anticipated. Yet, there was a part of her that understood the need to move on and accept the new dynamics of their lives. She vowed to focus on being the best mother she could be, and to give Nic's new relationship the space it needed to grow.

Watching Camila's car disappear down the road, Nic felt hopeful. He was optimistic that this conversation marked the beginning of a new chapter where Camila could accept his relationship with Celia, not just for his sake, but for the children's. The path ahead would undoubtedly have its challenges, but with patience and understanding, Nic was hopeful they could all find a way to coexist harmoniously.

During Celia's next visit to Virginia, Adrián sat on the couch, his eyes glued to his video game, barely acknowledging Celia as she entered the room. Celina, on the other hand, ran up to Celia with a bright smile.

"Hi, Celia! Did you bring the cookies you promised?" Celina asked, her eyes wide with excitement.

Celia knelt down to Celina's level, pulling a small tin from her bag. "Of course I did! Chocolate chip, just like you like them."

Celina clapped her hands in delight, but Adrián remained silent, his fingers tapping furiously on the controller. Celia glanced at him, her smile faltering slightly.

"Adrián, I was thinking we could all go to the park later. What do you think?" Celia asked, trying to engage him.

Adrián shrugged, not looking up. "Whatever."

Nic, watching from the doorway, sighed and walked over to his son. "Hey, bud, give it a chance. It could be fun."

Adrián finally looked up, his eyes meeting Celia's. There was a flicker of something—curiosity, perhaps—but he quickly masked it with indifference. "Fine. I'll go."

Celina, oblivious to the tension, grabbed Celia's hand. "Let's go now! I want to show you the swings!"

As they headed out, Nic placed a reassuring hand on Celia's shoulder. "It'll take time, but they'll come around."

Celia nodded, her smile returning as she squeezed Nic's hand. "I hope so."

Celia understood that her role in Nic's life was not only as his partner but as a supportive presence for his children. She was determined to build trust and create a harmonious environment where Adrián and Celina could feel secure and loved. Her journey with Nic was about blending their lives while respecting the past and embracing the future.

The new reality they faced was one of change and adaptation. Camila, Nic, and Celia had all taken significant steps toward finding closure and moving on from their tumultuous past. In the midst of their struggles, there was a shared commitment to providing a stable and loving environment for the children. Each of them knew that the journey ahead would require continuous effort, understanding, and a willingness to put the past behind them.

As they navigated this new chapter of their lives, Camila, Nic, and Celia found solace in the realization that moving on didn't mean forgetting. It meant embracing the lessons learned, finding peace in new beginnings, and fostering a future where their children could thrive. Together, albeit on separate paths, they were determined to create a reality where happiness and closure were not just possible, but within reach.

While their individual journeys were far from easy, they each recognized the importance of their new roles. Camila focused on being the best mother she could be, Nic embraced his renewed sense of self-worth, and Celia integrated herself into the family with care and respect. Despite the pain and challenges, there was hope that they could form a supportive network for the sake of the children.

In the end, it wasn't just about moving on—it was about moving forward, together, in their own ways. They knew that by working collaboratively and prioritizing the children's well-being, they could build a future where their children felt loved, secure, and ready to embrace their own paths.

CHAPTER 21
STRADDLING TWO WORLDS

Celia's relationship with Nic was filled with love and support. However, Camila complicated it. At school events, Nic always acknowledged her role in their children's lives, giving her the rightful place. While Celia understood and respected this, it often left her feeling ostracized and jealous.

Standing at the edge of the playground, Celia nervously twisted the strap of her purse. She watched as Nic and Camila chatted animatedly with the other parents, their laughter ringing out across the yard. Celia forced a smile when Adrián waved at her, but inside, she felt like an intruder in her own life. Whenever Nic attended school events where Camila was present, Celia couldn't help but feel a pang of insecurity. She knew that Nic's actions were out of respect for Camila's position as the children's mother, but it didn't make the situation any easier. She felt like an outsider, struggling to find her place in the family dynamics.

Despite these feelings, Celia remained committed to building a strong bond with Nic's children. She continued to be engaging and supportive, even when it was difficult. Adrián's comment about wishing his mother were more like her was a bittersweet reminder of the impact she was making, even if it wasn't always visible. Celia understood that integrating into this family meant walking a tightrope between being a supportive partner to Nic and respecting Camila's role. She often felt caught in the middle, striving to create a harmonious environment for the children while managing her own feelings of jealousy and isolation.

Every smile from the kids and every small moment of connection gave her hope, but the underlying tension never completely disappeared. Celia longed for acceptance, not just from Nic and the children, but from the entire family dynamic. She hoped that, in time, her dedication and love would help bridge the gap, allowing her to find her place and feel truly at home.

Celia and Nic had many conversations about these feelings. One evening at home, Celia confessed, "I know you're just trying to be respectful to Camila, but sometimes it feels like I'm invisible when she's around."

"I'm sorry, Celia. I never want you to feel that way. It's just... complicated. Camila is the kids' mother, and I don't want to undermine her role," Nic explained.

"I understand that, but where does that leave me? I'm trying so hard to be a part of this family, but it feels like I'm always on the outside looking in," Celia said, her voice filled with frustration.

"You're not on the outside. You're a crucial part of this family. We'll figure this out together, I promise," Nic reassured her.

Through open communication and mutual support, Celia and Nic navigated the complexities of their blended family. It wasn't always easy, but their dedication to each other and the children helped them overcome the obstacles. Celia's journey of personal growth and her efforts to integrate into the family continued, bringing them all closer together.

Celia lay awake that night, staring at the ceiling. She replayed the day's events in her mind, the way Nic's eyes lit up when he saw Camila, the way he seemed to forget she was even there. She loved Nic and the kids, but sometimes she wondered if she would ever truly belong in this family.

Nic felt like he was straddling two worlds. Camila often complained about feeling like an outsider in her children's lives now that they had a 'stepmom.' This added another layer of complexity to Nic's already challenging situation. He found himself caught between trying to honor Camila's role as the children's mother and supporting Celia as she integrated into their family.

Camila struggled with the children always talking about Celia. Her jealousy festered, secretly hoping that if things became too hard for Celia, she and Nic would break up. Camila would purposely undermine

Celia, making subtle comments to the children and Nic that cast doubt on Celia's place in their lives.

One evening, Camila confronted Nic, her voice tinged with hurt. "I overheard Adrián tell Celina that he wished I was more like Celia. Are you trying to replace me?" Camila's eyes were filled with pain.

"No, Camila. Celia is just trying to be supportive. Adrián didn't mean it that way," Nic replied, trying to calm the situation.

"It doesn't feel that way. I'm their mother, Nic. I shouldn't have to compete for their affection," Camila insisted. "Why does Celia have to attend the children's events? I'm here to support them. All they need is their mother and their father."

"You're not competing. The kids love you both. We need to find a way to make this work without anyone feeling left out," Nic said, hoping to find a resolution.

Camila's heart ached with a mix of jealousy and sadness. She felt as though she was being replaced, her role as the children's mother diminishing in the presence of Celia. Despite Nic's reassurances, the fear of losing her children's affection lingered. She realized that navigating this new reality required her to accept the changes and find a way to coexist, but the path ahead seemed daunting and uncertain. Camila couldn't help but reflect on the past, wishing she had known that her actions years ago would lead to such difficult consequences. She now faced the challenge of moving forward and finding her place within this altered family dynamic.

Nic watched Celia from across the room, her forced smile not reaching her eyes. He knew she was struggling, and it tore him apart. He loved her deeply, but balancing the needs of his children, Camila, and Celia felt like an impossible task. He just hoped he could find a way to make everyone feel valued.

The constant tension left Nic questioning whether the relationship was worth it. He loved Celia deeply, but dealing with the emotional turmoil from both women was exhausting. He often thought to himself, "If only there was a manual for this. Blended Families for Dummies, anyone?"

Despite these challenges, Nic knew that open communication was key. He had honest conversations with both Camila and Celia, trying to address their concerns and find a balance. He reassured Camila that her place in the children's lives was irreplaceable, while also supporting Celia in her efforts to build a strong bond with the kids.

Through these efforts, Nic hoped to create a harmonious environment for everyone involved. It wasn't easy, but his commitment to his family and his love for Celia kept him going. He believed that with patience and understanding, they could navigate the complexities of their blended family and find a way to coexist peacefully.

As they continued to navigate this journey, each step brought its own challenges and triumphs. For Camila, it was about letting go of the past and embracing her role as a co-parent. For Celia, it was finding her place in a family that wasn't originally hers, while building strong relationships with Nic and his children. And for Nic, it was about balancing these dynamics with compassion and patience.

In the end, their efforts started to pay off. Small moments of laughter, shared joys, and heartfelt conversations became more frequent. The path wasn't without its hurdles, but together, they found a way to make it work. The new reality of their lives may have been complex, but it was also filled with hope and the promise of a brighter future for everyone involved.

CHAPTER 22
FLOURISHING APART

Nic stood at the threshold of a new chapter in his life, the echoes of his past still lingering but no longer defining him. His decision to stop drinking, focus on his career, and invest in self-improvement marked the beginning of a transformative journey. He was determined to rebuild not just for himself, but for his children, who deserved a stable and loving home.

Standing in the doorway of his newly renovated home, Nic felt a sense of pride. The house, once filled with tension and conflict, now radiated warmth and positivity. The walls were painted in soft, inviting colors, and the rooms were filled with light and laughter. These changes were hard, but they were necessary to create a better life for his children and himself.

One evening, as he sat in his home office, Nic received an email from his boss. He had been selected to lead a major project, a testament to his skills and leadership. It was a moment of triumph, symbolizing how far he had come. Nic's thoughts drifted to the past, to the years of struggle and conflict with Camila. It was as if the relationship had been holding him down, clouding his life with negative energy. But now, the house was a place of healing and growth, a sanctuary for him and his children.

As he walked through the house, Nic felt a sense of peace. The laughter of his children echoed through the halls, a reminder of the joy and love that filled their lives. He knew the journey was far from over, but he was ready to face whatever came next with strength and resilience.

Nic stepped out into the evening, the air cool against his skin. He looked at the house, its value doubled, not just in monetary terms, but in the happiness and stability it represented. He had created a new beginning for his family and was proud of the man he had become.

Sitting in his home office, reviewing the latest appraisal of his house, Nic reflected on how far he had come. The value had doubled since he bought it, a testament to the improvements he had made and the thriving neighborhood. The promotion he received at work came with a significant raise, allowing him to invest in his children's future and secure their financial stability.

Nic realized that the separation from Camila had been a turning point. Without the constant stress of managing her crises, he had focused on his career and personal growth. Their relationship had held both of them back. Nic had become accustomed to managing her crises, which in hindsight was managing a toxic relationship. His love for Camila led him to enable her negative behaviors. Whenever she found herself in trouble—after a night of heavy drinking or neglecting household chores—Nic was there to help her. This allowed Camila to avoid facing the consequences of her behavior, hindering her growth and preventing her from taking responsibility for her life.

Camila had become increasingly dependent on Nic to fix her problems. This cycle left Nic emotionally and physically drained, unable to focus on his own needs and aspirations. The exhaustion affected his work performance and his ability to be fully present for their children, Adrián and Celina. The weight of Camila's problems became a heavy burden that Nic carried alone, leaving him feeling depleted and overwhelmed.

Camila resented the suburban lifestyle and its accompanying responsibilities. The home, once a place of comfort, became a battleground of unspoken resentments and unfulfilled needs.

Their relationship was unbalanced, lacking mutual support and understanding. Nic was always the caretaker, the one who held everything together, while Camila was the one needing care. This imbalance created resentment on both sides. Nic felt unappreciated and overburdened, his efforts to maintain stability going unnoticed. Camila felt controlled and misunderstood, her cries for help masked by her destructive actions.

Focused on managing immediate crises, both Nic and Camila missed opportunities for personal growth and fulfillment. They were stuck in a cycle of dysfunction that prevented them from achieving their potential. The constant firefighting left no room for self-reflection or improvement, trapping them in a toxic dynamic that neither knew how to escape.

Nic's journey of self-discovery and personal growth marked the end of a tumultuous chapter. By severing the ties of a toxic relationship, he found the space to heal and grow. His focus on creating a stable and loving environment for his children became his new purpose. With each step forward, Nic embraced the possibilities of a brighter future, ready to face the challenges ahead with resilience and hope.

Camila stood at the edge of the park, a place that held countless memories, both bitter and sweet, with Nic. The air was thick with memories of their toxic relationship, a bond that had once felt unbreakable but had ultimately suffocated them both. Their separation had been painful yet necessary, allowing them to grow individually and find their own paths.

Reflecting on their past, Camila realized how their issues had intertwined, creating a poisonous dynamic that brought out the worst in each other. Now, with the clarity that time and distance provided, she saw their breakup as a catalyst for personal growth, transforming their lives in ways they never imagined. Sitting at her kitchen table, a stack of bills and financial statements spread out before her, Camila felt a sense of control. The numbers, once intimidating, now represented empowerment. She had taken a financial counseling course and learned to manage her money. It wasn't easy, but it was empowering.

Glancing at her latest bank statement, Camila smiled. For the first time in years, her savings account showed a growing balance. She had paid off her credit card debt and was on track to clear her car loan. The sense of accomplishment was immense. Her phone buzzed with a message from her financial advisor, congratulating her on reaching her savings goal. A surge of pride washed over her. She had done this on her own, without needing Nic to bail her out.

What brought her the most pride was the ability to purchase her own home. No longer renting, she now had a small house where each child had their own bedroom and more room to play. It was a tangible symbol of her independence and growth. Camila had built a stable, loving environment for her children, proving to herself that she could create a new life for them.

Camila's journey of self-discovery and empowerment culminated in the purchase of that home. Standing at the edge of her property, she felt a deep sense of pride and accomplishment. Her journey had been filled with challenges, but she had emerged stronger and more resilient, ready to embrace the future with confidence.

Separation is never easy, but sometimes it becomes the catalyst for profound personal growth and transformation. For Nic and Camila, parting ways had been a painful yet necessary step to break free from the toxic cycle that had consumed their relationship. The separation allowed them both to discover their strengths, focus on self-improvement, and build better lives for themselves and their children.

One evening, as they exchanged their children for the weekend, Camila and Nic shared a brief conversation.

"You know, it's ironic," Camila said, a hint of a smile on her lips. "We struggled so much together, but we've both done better on our own."

Nic nodded, a thoughtful expression crossing his face. "I guess we were enabling each other in the worst ways. Remember how we used to argue about money all the time? It feels like a lifetime ago."

Camila sighed, her eyes reflecting a mix of regret and understanding. "Yeah, I remember. I was so irresponsible with our finances, and you always tried to fix everything. It wasn't fair to you or the kids."

Nic's gaze softened as he looked at her. "We both made mistakes. I thought I was helping by taking on all the burdens, but I was just making things worse. It took the separation for me to see that."

Camila nodded, a sense of mutual understanding passing between them. "I'm glad we're both doing well now. For the kids' sake, and for ourselves. Therapy helped me recognize my patterns and work on them. I've learned to stand on my own two feet."

Nic smiled, genuine warmth in his eyes. "And I've learned to focus on my own growth too. Leading that project at work and getting the promotion was a turning point for me. It showed me what I'm capable of when I'm not constantly stressed."

Camila's smile widened. "We've come a long way, haven't we? I'm proud of us. We've both grown so much."

Nic nodded, feeling a sense of closure. "Me too. We've created better lives for ourselves and the kids. It wasn't easy, but it was worth it."

As they parted ways, both felt a sense of peace. They had found their paths to financial independence and personal responsibility and, in doing so, discovered their own strengths. Their separation had become a catalyst for growth, allowing them to blossom in ways they never could have together.

CHAPTER 23
A NEW BEGINNING

Nic and Celia's relationship blossomed in the aftermath of turmoil and heartbreak, a testament to their resilience and the power of new beginnings. From their first meeting at a beachside bar, there was an undeniable connection—a spark neither of them could ignore. Over time, their bond deepened, developing into a partnership built on trust, respect, and mutual support.

At first, Nic was reluctant to commit, still haunted by the trauma of his past. While Celia was ready to take their relationship to the next level, Nic needed time to fully heal. This difference created tension, but Celia's patience and understanding allowed him to process his feelings at his own pace.

As Nic healed, he found himself opening up to Celia in ways he hadn't with anyone else. Her empathy created a safe space for him to express his fears and vulnerabilities. She stood by him through the challenges, offering unwavering support and encouragement. Together, they navigated the complexities of blending their lives, finding joy in the small moments and strength in their shared experiences.

Celia's relationship with Adrián and Celina also flourished. She dedicated herself to building a positive connection with them, respecting Nic and Camila's roles while creating her own special place in their hearts. The children, initially cautious, slowly embraced Celia's presence. Her patience and genuine care helped bridge the gap, fostering a sense of trust and acceptance. They began to see her as a significant and positive influence, adding to the family's happiness.

Nic and Celia's love for travel and adventure brought them closer, creating lasting memories and strengthening their bond. From weekend getaways to exploring new places, each journey was a testament to their commitment to building a future filled with love and happiness.

Their home became a sanctuary of warmth and laughter, a space where love thrived, and every corner reflected their shared dreams and aspirations. Their relationship was far from perfect, but it was real and grounded in a deep understanding of each other's pasts and hopes for the future.

As years passed, Nic's fears faded. He realized his reluctance had been rooted in past pain, and he finally found the courage to fully commit to Celia. Surrounded by close family and friends, they exchanged vows, promising to support each other through life's highs and lows. This new chapter in Nic's life symbolized his complete healing from the trauma of betrayal. He had found love again, built on a foundation of trust and mutual respect.

Nic's marriage to Celia showed that even after the darkest times, one could find light and love again. As he became more emotionally available and open, his relationship with Celia flourished. Free from the shadows of his past, he was a better partner and father. Forgiving Camila didn't mean forgetting the hurt but choosing to focus on the positive aspects of his life and the love he had found.

Celia and Camila would never be best friends, but they learned to work together for the children's sake. Their interactions, initially awkward, gradually found a rhythm. They communicated clearly about schedules and events, ensuring Adrián and Celina felt supported and loved by both households.

Nic no longer felt he was straddling two worlds. The initial tension between Celia and Camila had softened into mutual understanding. Both women recognized the importance of their roles in the children's lives and worked to maintain a respectful and cooperative relationship. This newfound harmony brought Nic a sense of relief and stability, allowing him to fully embrace his life with Celia without the constant pull of unresolved conflicts.

Together, they created an environment where the children could thrive, surrounded by love and understanding from both sides. This cooperative co-parenting dynamic was a testament to their shared commitment to Adrián and Celina's well-being, proving that even complex relationships could evolve into a balanced and supportive system.

Nic and Celia continued to support each other's growth. They faced challenges with grace, celebrated successes with joy, and navigated life's uncertainties with unwavering faith in their love. Their journey was a testament to the transformative power of compassion, understanding, and the belief that even after the darkest times, there is always the possibility of a brighter tomorrow.

Their story was one of resilience, love, and unwavering dedication to building a life together. Despite the challenges and growth they faced, they found strength in each other. As they stood side by side, ready to face whatever the future held, they knew their love had been forged in the fires of adversity, making it all the more precious. With Adrián and Celina happily embracing the new family dynamics and a harmonious relationship with Camila, they looked forward to a future filled with hope, joy, and endless possibilities. In the end, Nic and Celia proved that no matter how dark the past, new beginnings always bring the promise of a brighter tomorrow.

CHAPTER 24
EMBRACING SELF-FORGIVENESS

Camila sat alone in her house, haunted by past mistakes and the memory of Nic, who had once loved her unconditionally. Her life had turned into a series of fleeting relationships, each more disillusioning than the one before. Her struggles with guilt and self-worth caused her relationships to crumble. She watched friends build meaningful lives while she remained stuck in superficial connections, her past choices a chain around her neck. Despite therapy and support groups, regret remained her constant companion.

When she heard about Nic and Celia's marriage, a flood of emotions overwhelmed her. The news was a stark reminder of what she had lost. Jealousy, hurt, and resentment mingled with a deep sense of failure. Camila knew that Nic had found the stability and happiness she had once sabotaged. The thought of Celia stepping into a role she once held was a bitter pill to swallow.

Camila's mind replayed the moments leading up to their separation, wishing she had made different choices. She couldn't escape the feeling that her actions years ago had led to this moment of isolation and regret. Nic had moved on, building a new life filled with love and support, while she remained stuck in the past, unable to find her footing.

She realized that moving forward required her to confront her past and accept the consequences of her actions. The path ahead seemed daunting, but she knew that healing was a journey she had to undertake. Her regret served as a reminder of the importance of making better choices, not just for herself, but for the possibility of a brighter future.

Her once-powerful vanity now left her hollow and regretful. Her pride had always been her beauty, which she wielded like a weapon. Over the years, she gained weight, and her prized beauty faded. No amount of makeup or luxury facials could hide the toll of time and regret etched onto her face.

As the years passed, Camila's life became a tapestry threaded with regret. Each decision she made, each moment she chose thrill over stability, added to the heavy burden she carried. Happy families in the park, parents playing with their children—all gave her a pang of longing. She remembered the early days with Nic, the dreams they had shared, and the love that had once seemed unbreakable.

A turning point came at a college reunion. As friends reminisced, Camila realized how much her life had diverged from the path she had envisioned. Her friends spoke of their families and careers with fulfillment, while Camila felt a deep emptiness. She had chased excitement and thrills, but in doing so, she had lost the things that truly mattered.

Camila's regret affected her relationships. She found it difficult to connect with others on a meaningful level, often sabotaging her own happiness due to feelings of guilt and unworthiness. Superficial connections only left her feeling more isolated and alone. She longed for the deep connection she had once had with Nic—a bond built on mutual trust, respect, and emotional intimacy. Camila knew that kind of relationship was a once-in-a-lifetime occurrence, and having squandered it, she feared she might never find it again.

Now in her mid-40s, Camila had settled into a quieter life. She found peace in her job, where she was respected and valued for her skills. She made new friends, built a support system, and cautiously began dating again. The pain of the past lingered, but it became a part of her story—a chapter in the book of her life.

Her relationship with her children was far from perfect, and she knew she would never have the same special place in their hearts as Nic did. In the beginning, Adrián and Celina had been reluctant to spend time with her, often expressing their preference to stay with Nic. The initial days were filled with tense interactions and strained conversations, but Camila remained patient and consistent. She attended their school events, helped with homework, and made an effort to be present in their lives.

Over time, her genuine care and dedication began to soften their resistance. They started to open up to her, sharing their thoughts and feelings more freely. While Nic still held a special place in their hearts, Camila cherished the bond they were building. Their relationship grew meaningful and filled with mutual respect, a testament to her growth and the love she had for her children, despite the rocky start.

Determined not to repeat her mistakes, Camila found acceptance, realizing that life didn't always go as planned. True happiness came not from a perfect life but from embracing imperfections and finding strength in adversity. Looking ahead, she felt hope—a sense that the future held new beginnings, and despite the pain of the past, there was always the possibility of a brighter tomorrow.

Her journey from a loving wife and mother to a woman grappling with the consequences of her choices, and ultimately finding a new path, highlighted the resilience of the human spirit. It showed how a seemingly perfect life can fall apart when faced with temptation and betrayal. While the scars of her past remained, she emerged stronger, wiser, and more determined to build a life of integrity and fulfillment.

One afternoon, browsing online for a book to read, she stumbled upon a novel she had read years ago. The story of betrayal and redemption, of a woman rebuilding her life from ashes, resonated deeply. The protagonist's journey mirrored her own.

That evening, she bought a blank notebook and began to write. She poured her thoughts, memories, and reflections onto its pages—the early days of her marriage, the love, the unraveling, and the betrayal. Writing became her therapy, a way to process lingering emotions. She wrote late into the night, losing track of time. Words flowed until peace settled over her, a peace she hadn't known before.

Though she never found another relationship as meaningful as with Nic, Camila learned to find solace in her own company. She embraced the lessons of her past, striving to be a better person each day. Her journey became one of self-discovery and acceptance, a life now guided by integrity and compassion.

Seeking new purpose, Camila began volunteering at a women's center helping others with similar struggles. Sharing her story brought a sense of redemption. This work gave her fulfillment and allowed her to use her experiences to make a positive impact. While she could never undo the past, she found solace in knowing she could still make a difference.

One night, as she finished another entry, Camila realized that through her writing, she had created a new narrative—one of strength, resilience, and self-discovery. The blank pages had transformed into a testament of her journey, a beacon of hope and inner power. She closed the notebook, not with a sense of finality but with the understanding that this was just the beginning of a new chapter in her life.

Embracing her newfound wisdom, Camila looked forward with a renewed sense of purpose, ready to face whatever came next with grace and courage.

CHAPTER 25

THE POWER OF FORGIVENESS

Nic sat in his favorite chair as the evening light cast long shadows across the room. The house was quiet—a stark contrast to the past chaos. Glancing at a photo of his children on the mantel, he felt a surge of love and joy that had sustained him through the toughest times.

The betrayal had left him bitter and angry, making trust difficult. He focused on his children, determined to be the best father he could despite the pain of Camila's betrayal. For their sake, he and Camila maintained a cordial relationship. They attended school events together, celebrated birthdays as a family, and tried to create a sense of normalcy for Adrián and Celina. But the wounds ran deep, and the connection they once shared had vanished.

Forgiving Camila hadn't been easy. The pain of her betrayal, the sleepless nights, and the burden of raising their children alone left scars. Yet, over the years, Nic realized that holding onto anger only harmed him. Letting go became necessary—not for Camila's sake, but for his own peace.

His journey toward forgiveness was gradual, marked by small steps. He acknowledged her efforts to change, recognized her struggles, and understood her remorse. He saw her trying to make amends. While he couldn't erase the past, he chose to move beyond it.

Through journaling, Camila realized she needed to offer Nic a genuine apology. One evening, as she dropped off the kids, they found themselves alone in the kitchen while the children were already upstairs.

"How are you?" Nic asked gently.

Camila smiled, genuinely content. "I'm doing well. I'm happy."

Nic nodded, his expression softening. "Me too."

They stood there for a moment—two people who had once been everything to each other, now simply acquaintances with a shared past. There was no bitterness or regret, just peace.

"Nic, I need to say something important for my growth and for our future. This has been weighing on me," Camila said. "I need to express it to move forward genuinely."

"Let's sit at the table," he said, starting a pot of tea.

They sat down for a long-overdue conversation, the kitchen thick with raw emotions and unspoken memories. "I know I can't undo the past," Camila began, tears streaming down her face. "But I need you to know how deeply sorry I am—for everything. For hurting you, for hurting the kids. Making amends isn't just about my recovery; it's about taking responsibility for the pain I've caused."

Nic sat in silence, his mind racing through memories of lonely nights and consuming anger, of times when forgiveness felt impossible. Yet, he also remembered the love they'd shared and the family they'd built. Letting go of his resentment felt like shedding a heavy coat he'd worn for too long.

"I appreciate that, Camila," he said slowly, each word weighed. "It's taken me a long time to reach this point, but I want to forgive you—not just for your sake, but for mine. This anger... it's not helping anyone anymore."

Camila waited, a mix of relief and fear in her eyes. Seeing Nic's pain made her past regrets pale beside the reality of the hurt she'd caused. His willingness to forgive offered a glimmer of hope that they could rebuild something new.

The evening light shifted, casting a warm glow that seemed to guide Nic toward peace. For Camila, his forgiveness validated her efforts to change, reassuring her she was on the right path. Though their romantic relationship had ended, they began building something different—a connection rooted in mutual respect and dedication to their children.

The conversation ended naturally. At the door, they exchanged brief, understanding smiles. "Goodnight, Camila," Nic said softly.

"Goodnight, Nic," she replied, her voice filled with newfound hope.

Driving back to her apartment, Camila felt a burden lift from her shoulders. The past was behind her, and the future beckoned. Though painful, the journey had led to growth and self-discovery. Whatever challenges lay ahead, she felt ready to face them.

In his quiet kitchen, Nic reflected. The house no longer felt empty, but rather filled with a peace he hadn't known before. Forgiving Camila wasn't just about releasing the past—it was about embracing possibility. The warm evening glow marked a new beginning.

Forgiveness opened the door to deeper healing. By letting go of bitterness, he could fully embrace his present life. His relationship with Celia flourished as he became more emotionally available. Free from past shadows, he grew into a better partner and father. Forgiveness didn't mean forgetting; it meant choosing to focus on the love and joy in his life now.

As the years passed, Nic and Camila found their new normal. Adrián and Celina grew into resilient children, despite their challenges. Camila and Nic developed a strong co-parenting relationship, always putting their children first.

Nic's forgiveness helped his children rebuild their relationship with their mother, teaching them resilience and family bonds. His story demonstrated remarkable grace, especially in a community where machismo often dictated responses to betrayal. Above all, he ensured Adrián and Celina felt secure and loved through every change, prioritizing their well-being over his own emotions.

Nic's choice to forgive Camila, despite the pain she caused, was pivotal. It showcased his profound capacity for compassion, transforming what could have been a tale of bitterness into one of redemption and growth. Through his actions, Nic demonstrated that true strength lies not in retaliation, but in compassion, understanding, and unwavering love. His journey reminds us that even in dark times, we can choose to act with integrity and grace.

Through his unwavering dedication to his children, Nic provided a foundation for rebuilding their lives. His strength, forgiveness, and commitment showed that true power lies in the ability to forgive and to prioritize the well-being of those we love. His story underscores the transformative power of grace and the potential for healing and new beginnings, even after the deepest wounds.

Though Camila and Nic went their separate ways, their journeys remained intertwined by the lessons they learned. Nic found happiness with Celia, and Camila discovered a renewed sense of purpose. Both grew from their experiences, understanding what truly mattered. Their journey toward forgiveness and redemption was a testament to healing and personal growth. They learned that while the past couldn't be changed, the future was theirs to shape. Through forgiveness, they found a way forward, creating a new chapter filled with hope and possibility.

Nic's forgiveness didn't just heal his past; it opened his heart to a future with Celia. Their love flourished, and they decided to expand their family. One evening, Nic and Celia prepared a special dinner to share the exciting news with Adrián and Celina. As they sat around the table, Nic looked at Celia, her smile filled with joy and anticipation.

"Kids, we have something very special to tell you," Nic began, his voice filled with excitement.

Celia squeezed Nic's hand and continued, "We're going to have a baby. You're going to have a little brother or sister."

Adrián and Celina's eyes widened in surprise. After a moment of silence, they both broke into smiles. "Really? A baby?" Adrián exclaimed.

Celina, with tears of joy in her eyes, jumped up to hug Celia. "That's amazing! I can't wait to be a big sister!"

As they celebrated the news, Nic felt a profound sense of happiness and fulfillment. His journey from betrayal and heartache to forgiveness and new beginnings had brought him to this moment. Surrounded by his loving family, he knew that the future held endless possibilities, and he was ready to embrace every one of them.

Nic and Camila's story stands as a powerful testament to the healing power of forgiveness, compassion, and unwavering dedication to what truly matters. Through their journey, they found peace, purpose, and the strength to move forward. Adrián and Celina thrived in an environment filled with love and stability. As a family, they created a future brimming with hope and possibilities. Even in the darkest times, they proved that there is always a chance for new beginnings and a brighter tomorrow.

As the final page turns, we are reminded that life is a journey filled with both triumphs and trials. Nic and Camila's paths diverged, yet through forgiveness and personal growth, they each found their way to a brighter future. Their story is a beacon of hope, demonstrating that even after the deepest wounds, it is possible to heal and find joy once more.

No matter the challenges you face or the mistakes you make, there is always an opportunity to start anew. Embrace forgiveness, cherish the moments that bring joy, and hold on to the belief that every end is but a beginning in disguise. The power to shape your future lies within your hands. With compassion and resilience, you can overcome any obstacle and emerge stronger. Remember, it's never too late to change your story or to transform adversity into triumph.

This story is a testament to the strength of the human spirit and the boundless capacity for growth and redemption. The journeys of Nic, Camila, Celia, Marcos, and the children reflect the complexities of life and the power of resilience. May their experiences inspire you to find your own path to happiness and fulfillment. Believe in the possibility of new beginnings, for it is through the challenges we face that we truly discover our potential. Let this story remind you that every step forward, no matter how small, brings you closer to a brighter, more hopeful future.

BLANCA DE LA ROSA: BIOGRAPHY

Blanca De La Rosa, born in the Dominican Republic and raised in the projects of the upper west side of Manhattan, is the daughter of Dominican immigrants. Despite cultural and linguistic challenges, she graduated from Pace University with a degree in international business management. She built a successful 34-year career at Mobil Oil and later ExxonMobil Oil Corporation, rising through various domestic and international roles that took her across the US, Europe, Central/South America, and Nigeria.

As a business development manager and president of the company's Employee Resource Group, De La Rosa represented ExxonMobil at the Hispanic Heritage Foundation's Regional and National Scholarship Awards. She also served as a host, keynote speaker, and panelist at numerous events supported by the company's charity foundation. Her most rewarding role was mentoring younger employees through the corporate maze.

De La Rosa is a self-published author:

Self-help and Career: "Empower Yourself for an Amazing Career" and "A Holistic Approach to Your Career," sharing career advice based on her successes. She combines practical, common-sense advice with inner wisdom and spirituality to provide strategies for workplace success.

Memoir/Autobiography: "Pursuing a Better Tomorrow" is an inspiring journey from Spain to the US, intertwining four stories that illustrate the challenges and opportunities of immigration, acculturation, coming of age, and self-discovery. De La Rosa shares her personal journey from New York City's projects to corporate America, highlighting her growth and achievements despite numerous challenges.

Self-help and Spiritual genre: "Your Power Within – Inner Guidance" explores themes of personal growth, the soul's journey, inner strength, and the quest for purpose. The book emphasizes patience and gradual progress, guiding readers toward understanding and evolving through their experiences.

BLANCA DE LA ROSA: BIBLIOGRAPHY

Self-Help / Spiritual

"Your Power Within—Inner Guidance" is a journey of self-discovery and healing. Through personal anecdotes and reflections, the book explores the quest for purpose and inner strength. It encourages readers to tap into their inner power, break free from limits, and create their dream life. This guide helps readers discover their passions, connect with their inner selves, and align with their greater purpose. Your inner power is limitless!

Self-Help / Career

A holistic approach is essential for upward mobility. Develop a career plan with clear goals and a forward-looking perspective.

Empower Yourself provides uplifting and inspiring insights. with practical advice and inner wisdom for workplace success.

Memoir / Autobiography

What would you give up today for a better tomorrow? This question fuels an inspiring cross-generational journey from Spain to the US, spanning over 100 years. Through the characters' stories, we see the challenges and opportunities of immigration, acculturation, coming of age, and self-discovery. De La Rosa's transition from New York City's projects to corporate America highlights her personal and professional growth.